Purdy Hous

D

To all my spooky family who are afraid of the dark and enter anyway!

Sufani Weisman-Garza

1377 Rikoppe Lane Reviews (Book I)

"Fully Enjoyed This Ghost Story. If you're looking for a horror book, the perfect chiller, this one is for you!"

~Beth, Bookstagram

"This Was My First Ever Horror Book and Boy Did It Live Up To My Expectations. I literally could not put this book down, so much so I made myself some popcorn while reading it as I was visualizing it playing out like a movie, as I was reading it. I literally got chills! I absolutely loved the characters. I'm already so excited for the next book in the series!!"

~LD, goodreads

"Absolutely LOVED This book!! It draws you in quick and gets better with every chapter you read. I literally could not put this book down. I had to keep reading. The ending was the best of any book I have ever read. I can't wait for the sequel.

~SD, Amazon

"Fun, Engaging Read. How can one say a horror story is fun? Well, this one is. And for people who live in the NW, the setting in Gig Harbor makes it more intriguing. I

4

couldn't put it down once I started. There are lots of ins and outs to the story and the house involved! It's a great lose-yourself read."

~AR, Amazon

"Love It! The story sucks you in until the very end. I hope there will be a sequel!!!

~GC, Amazon

Table of Contents

Sufani Weisman-Garza

Sufani Weisman-Garza

10

Chapter One

Reckoning

Remembering back to that morning in Fall, it was October, almost Halloween time and the weather was beginning to get chilly. Her husband Clay, the night before, was taken down from the clothes post in their closet, hung from his neck and his face, his lips, an ugly shade of black, purple, and blue that she would never get out of her head. His death, just as unnatural. It was the moment her personal hell began. Her descent into disbelief, darkness, and grief, yet fighting for the light.

Although the destruction was mammoth, and love abounded in friendship and sincere well wishes, she could not stand one more nicety, or, *Sorry for your loss*. Like a body in flight response, so too did her drive to leave it all behind, and she did just that!

Months had passed, their condo sold, and she found herself in the car, twisting and turning up a gently winding road, and felt a sense of peace in the storm that she hadn't felt in a while. She was a zombie then. She thought she had escaped the cloud around her life of sadness, shock, grief, and terror of suddenly realizing everything she thought her

11

life was, had changed overnight. He was gone, and with it their life.

But she had escaped nothing. The house she bought was beautiful, Victorian … and terrifying! It started the very first night, shadows that moved in the dark, items going missing or moved, lights flickering, escalating to being thrown, strange time warps, bad feelings, fear in her body for no reason, and dogs alerting her to a strange energy in the room. The house had come alive, talking to her through dreams, psychological mind games and bodily harm. The home was filled with spirits competing for her attention, some to tell her the truth, and one to hide it.

The gruesome discovery of the secret room in her home peaked with activity, more aligned with spiritual warfare. A child killer, dressing her murdered babies and toddlers like dolls after the kill, sewn mouths and eyes, teeth ripped from their mouths that one could only hope was done postmortem, the alternative too heinous to think of. The parents, once blamed for her death, perhaps were murdered victims themselves. What happened once they made the discovery that their daughter was a devil? If only the walls could talk. Much was deduced, but much still was – and would always remain – a mystery. The little demon child was revealed and oh did she rage. In that final moment of discovery, teeth poured from the ceiling into

12

the living room defying reality and logic, yet it happened. The same ceiling that connected her room and secret death chamber we now call the Cold Room.

Now, with a frozen gaze, looking out the kitchen window, she wondered why her life had become a continual fractal falling into tones, descending, down, and down? Life was once in the light, shining, all smiles. Why had she found herself in the tumult and feeling of continual dropping into an abyss, like a Shepard tone that never stops descending, no bottom, no end to the fall? It's a trick, that each descending bar allows one note to come up, keeping the forever falling tone. Has that become her life? Will she continue to drop into the abyss with no end or will she find her way out? Falling, falling, falling, this house, falling, these spirits, falling, falling, falling, falling, falling, falling into a family's hell! A family that is now somehow her family, if only by association, an association she never asked for nor wanted. Their family was cursed by a labyrinth of torment she could never know, or unknow, now that she knew such demented bliss came alive in the house she now owns. Falling, falling, falling! It was a trick, a trick, a trick; this Shepard tone! But the fucking portal of hell was real enough and now she had to live with it. What was she to

13

do with all this terror? How long could she be the one note always coming up?

Chapter Two
Teeth

The Universe speaks to us, are we listening? This whispering on the wind; what is it saying? This whispering: the endless whispering getting into my brain, coming from places I may not want to hear. All this whispering fills my mind and the shadows of those speaking words that fill this house. So, few living occupy this house, so many dead litter its corridors. How can I ever unsee these halls and rooms with dead children? They never wanted to be here. They never intended to be phantoms of this mansion, hidden away, hung on the walls like dolls for a sinister child killer. They never intended their light to be the gloom of these hallways. We share a common nightmare, a thinly gated veil between the worlds. They are dead, what am I? Only half here in my grief and always partly on the other side. The spirits talk to me. They know what I see.

Finding dead children in a cleverly hidden room in my newly purchased old Victorian was not part of my life plan. But neither was my husband hanging himself in our luxury walk-in closet. What darkness has its grip on me? What did I do to deserve this? I came here to escape the dark bird of my grief, only to be captured by the whirlwind, a fierce blowing circumstance that has turned my life

15

upside down. This strange bird of grief has incorporated me into its murder, its flock.

What am I to do with this wreckage? Like a boat stranded in shallow waters and battered by the sea and time, I have taken up residence in this luxury liner of despair. The hope that it was to be of fresh air and cheerfulness now only made me face what I had been running from in the first place. This beauty, this place, this history of time gone by, yet perfectly preserved, has ensured my preservation in making me face myself and what my life has been. The exodus I took to avoid what I saw in that closet, what pain I felt, why it had happened at all is still present. Still, no answers, if I could just shield it in drapery and luxury wallpaper, hide it in carpets and fine linens, antique lamps, and tuck myself in to a time past, I could avoid my time period, avoid my pain, avoid why the hell my husband killed himself and left me alone in this big world. I don't understand, I will never understand. I'm angry, so fucking angry. Why did he do this to me? Didn't he know the destruction he would wreak on my life?

She took a deep breath and exhaled slowly to calm her nerves. She wondered how long it would take before pleasant thoughts were those that consumed her mind again. She had no answer.

16

Staring out of the kitchen window, snapping out of her internal storm cloud, she could see the blue hue of water in the distance and once again felt grateful to have this sight. After all that had happened in this house, she found it imperative to dig for all the remaining remnants in the form of documents left in the home to fully understand the Purdy House history, and why so many lost souls have been stuck in this place, or simply refuse to move on. Although she saw many make their leave, she feels the sludge of those who did not leave, who are remaining in the walls of their choosing, yet to reveal themselves. She could feel their darkness.

Washing the sink, she stared at the mason jar full of teeth on the windowsill, as it sat in front of her kitchen window. The police thought they got them all but so many pouring from the ceiling, well, their tough ivory splattered like cake batter on raised beaters. The police would not miss these, and she hadn't the heart to toss them out. They belonged to the innocent.

The sun shone on them with its sweet rays betraying what they really were. The beauty and brightness of the sun, an oxymoron to its sinister presence of being. She remembered the events that led up to the ceiling raining these God-awful relics of the past horrors of this house, seemingly from nowhere and in unrealistic over

17

abundance. That space in this house an evil child created, her laboratory of horror, never intended to be found. The Cold Room, she now called it. The town now calls it!

I am famous for all the wrong reasons; infamous. All those children, dead children, she thought to herself. Found in the secret catacombs of her house. *The poor children*. A small capture remains in this jar, a reminder of the unbelievable reality that occurred here. A deluge of porcelain rain of all those lost souls, in a pile on the floor, as if the portal of hell opened up underneath her, the Cold Room, to release the contents of horror for the last time. So many, it was unrealistic to the amount of death, as though the evil girl unleashed her joyful hell on her home – one they share in common now – and on her family, that day! If she did not capture what she saw, she knew she would one day look back and question her sanity that it happened at all. But she did capture those teeth from children who had them ripped from their mouths by a demented girl, a child herself, playing dentist like her father, knowing she was wrong, which is why she hid her work. Knowing it was wrong as she saw the mothers searching for their children, knowing she had killed them before their grief cried out. *What evil possessed such a child? I cannot see her as human, only, other!* What *other* possessed her, and why has it found shelter in this home, her home?

18

Sufani Weisman-Garza

The ominous truth of that day was in front of her face, mixed with sunshine of real life, present, though she could, even now, scarcely believe it happened at all.

Chapter Three
Mundane

Sitting in the kitchen at the small circular table, confined to this one space, she felt relatively safe in her own home. Although the kitchen was large with high ceilings and plenty of counter space, it remained cozy, separated from the more formal dining area. The delicate clink of the small spoon on the dainty cup was heard as she stirred her half packet of stevia into her favorite coffee. She sat alone at the table in the kitchen, the beam of sunlight from the world outside aiming directly at her in a line, as if calling her to wake up to her life again and not let this comedy of horrors that her life seemed to be piling up, become her life. She had a choice, the sun was saying to her, *choose life*, it whispered. The steam rose from her cup, and she lifted it to her lips in that thought and took a sip. *"Rejoin life,"* the whispers said!

As she thought about what the sun was saying, and the whispers were spoken silently, there was a knock at the door. She already knew who it was. The sound of men's knuckles on the back door could only be one person, and it wasn't the milkman. How was she so in tune with the house and the noises it made so distinctly to know the difference a woman's knuckles made against its antique

20

wood? How indeed, but she did, it was though she were wired in, like the electricity running silently and unseen through the house able to bring it to life and make it habitable. Like it or not, she was part of this house; it chose her in a strange way, as the caretaker of this time period. And despite her reluctance to accept what happened in her house, she wouldn't leave it either. The house needed her, and she needed this house. A twisted bond of darkness struggling to see the light, like her life, and her grief, with joy waiting to inhabit, if only the falling could stop.

"I knew it was you," she said to Dr. Donovan, now just her friend, not her therapist, as she opened the door.

"Of course it would be me. I had to check in on you, Jo," he said entering the house as she went back to sit at the table. "It's been a week. You haven't picked up my calls since the incident, and I am worried about you, " Dr. Donovan said.

"So, you're here as my therapist then?" she said in her usual matter-of-fact tone, being that originally he was her therapist for a very, very brief moment, until she decided he would be better suited as her friend. To her, he was more of a first connection to the town than someone she felt was a therapist for her. Not because he wasn't good, she just never felt connected to him that way,

Sufani Weisman-Garza

nor needed him in that manner. Her family were her therapy, slash, nags. She ended her sessions with him only after a few and naturally they became friends, seeing him around town all the time. He was a pillar of appropriateness, and also not bad on the eyes, in a clean shaven and neatly dressed Keanu Reeves sort of way. Most importantly, he was kind, and she needed a kind friend right about now.

"No, actually I came here to tell you in person that I'm recusing myself as your therapist."

She looked at him with eyebrows raised. Hadn't she kind of already dumped his therapy chair?

"I want to be your friend. Officially!" he said with a smile. "And … it *is* inappropriate to see you as a client when we are personally seeing each other," he said with a charming smile, flashing his teeth like a tooth paste commercial with that twinkle at the end from the shine.

Her eyebrows lifted again. Johannah smiled her notorious closed mouth smirk, "Well, you sure are taking liberties," she said shaking her head yes. "Seeing each other, huh?"

"We can talk about your liberties if you want too, but I would much rather just be here with you. Even if it is quietly. You've been through a lot. Could be nice to just sit with someone quietly and …" and Jo cut him off.

22

"When does the *quietly* part start?" she said and gave a smile and held her coffee to her lips, attempting to take a sip.

"Classic Jo. There she is," he said and smiled, sitting in the empty chair next to her. "Can I have a cup?" He moved the conversation along, knowing he didn't know a classic Jo, their friendship was new, yet it was so familiar and comfortable.

She pointed at the coffeepot, and he knew what to do. They sat quietly at the table, sipping their steaming coffee, and sharing that joyous sun beam in silence. Content!

The house didn't make a sound.

Chapter Four
Evil Still

After Donovan (Dr. D or DeeDee) left, she continued with the daily chores of the home and took in the odd quiet of the home.

"Nos-Ferrah-Tu," she called out, and all three of her loyal rescue bulldogs snorted their way to her playfully. Yes, they were named after her favorite creepy classic film, *Nosferatu*. She knelt down to their level and gave them all scratches. They were even cheerful as though they had been released from an invisible assailant. As much as she wanted to believe it and share their feelings, she was suspicious. Dogs had a wonderful way of being present.

"You guys ready to go for a walk? I know you can't go too far, but maybe just around the neighborhood?" They looked at her approvingly and she harnessed them all up and headed for the front door. Out they went, down the front stairs, away from the porch, the witch's cap, and the peering eyes of the front widows that watched her from the Cold Room. She didn't dare look up. She had enough of the Cold Room and wanted a few moments to just not think about it. But she felt what evil still lingered there. In her bones she felt it. You can ask a ghost to leave, but they will damn well do what they want, at the end of the day. The slightest drop of the drape caught from the corner of her eye was proof!

Chapter Five
Ain't No Pan Zees

"Hello?" Jo heard echoing from her bedroom upstairs. It was Layce down stairs, her voice reverberating off the incredible high ceilings and majestic Victorian walls. A home, or mausoleum? Perhaps both.

"Come on up. I'm in my room," Jo called out to her and there was a silence. She peeked her head out her bedroom door when the silence went on for a few more seconds. She saw Layce at the bottom of the stair entrance from the back of the house, looking up timidly with one foot on the first stair, one arm on the railing, and frozen.

Jo smiled, "It's okay, come on up."

"Are you sure," Layce said. "It still gives me the creeps."

"I know. Me too, but life goes on, Sista! And we ain't no pan zees."

"Yah, that's right. WE AIN'T NO PAN ZEES," she said loud like she was telling someone listening who shouldn't be there, puffing herself up and making a body building move, flexing and turning in a half-moon and back, puckering her lips like a duck, as she walked up the stairs and down the hallway to Jo's room.

Jo let out a laugh at her sister. "You're so goofy," and she smiled lovingly, walking back to the bed and folding her freshly cleaned t-shirts and putting them in the drawer.

"What's going on with you today," Layce asked as she plopped down on her bed, smiling at her sister until she got a glimpse of the door across the hall, the infamous "Cold Room" and made a gas face of distaste and her head slightly pulled back. She then carried on with her sister, hoping Jo didn't see her wince. Of course, she did but said nothing.

"I might go visit Geraldine over at the Historical Society and see if I can't get more information on Nina. Something is calling me to talk to her again," Jo finished.

"Who, Geraldine or Nina?" Layce asked.

"Nina." Jo motioned her to go with her back down stairs. Jo was leading and Layce pushed her way in front of her to be the farthest away from the Cold Room.

"Nice," Jo said sarcastically. "Nice to know what would happen in a real emergency," and they both laughed and took the back stairs to the kitchen. Layce always loved the kitchen, she loved eating Jo's food and drinking her beverages.

At the bottom of the stairs, they both looked over to the right before turning into the kitchen to see Mom's designated room, and both knew at the same time, they missed their mother. Lorna, Jo's mother had visited and was exposed to a terrifying experience that made her both defensive for Jo and also terrified. In an effort to keep her safe Jo sent her back home for the time being.

Layce, a free-spirited massage therapist was more than happy to move and be with her sister during this time to cheer her spirits and begin a new life. She had also taken a fancy to the local barista named Ginni and had stolen her away from her boyfriend Rico, who worked at the Ruff Times & Happy Endings Transitional Dog Spa and Rescue, where Jo got her dogs, Nos-Ferrah and Tu, named after her favorite scary classic, Nosferatu.

"I wonder what Mom is doing today," Layce asked.

"I wonder if Mom will come back after everything?" Jo asked.

They both took turns at the coffee pot making their pour quietly thinking, and hoping she would.

28

Chapter Six
Entering the Room

I don't know why I am drawn to that room. But I am. Maybe it is my orneriness, but this is my house, and I'll be damned if I let some little psycho girl keep me from enjoying my house. I'm not gonna lie, though, I am scared most nights in this place. Even in the day there is a strange fog at times in certain areas of the hallway leading to the back room. Some might call it morning glory, but from what I have seen happen in this hallway, there ain't nothing glorious about it!

I stand in front of the Cold Room door, fittingly nicknamed now, for its dark shadows and cold creepiness, despite what I have done to make it nice. I turn the knob and dare to go in, despite all my senses warning me not to.

"Cause this is my house, bitch," I say out loud to myself, in a hallway! No thought to any consequence I could feel for saying it, having been slapped and thrown in this very hallway before. Maybe I am fearless after all I have been through? To be honest, I have always been fearless in a sort of gentle way. I know who I am, and I own my power, and I never cower. I didn't mean that to rhyme, but there it is! Lol.

29

I enter the room and look at the beauty of it and look out the window. The one connection the room has to today's era and yet it seems like the room itself will not allow itself to be moved into this time period. Not because anyone living is trying to keep it locked in time. Plenty of homes purposefully use antiques to allow the experience of a lost generation, as I have done to continue its preservation. Not this room. This room has the same presence of a person, stubborn, and refusing to be led into this century. It is locked in time, in an angry sort of way and is not afraid to move things, shift temperatures, or manifest troubling things into any room in the house to make its point. It will not budge from the past.

I think to myself, *I shall do my best to not be like this room!*

A beautifully decorated room, rich velvet mauve and black wallpaper, dark wood, a huge window looking out into the world this room and its occupants were no longer part of, and she, where is she in all of this? It was almost as though the room were inciting her to become part of its never-ending play; to neither belong to this world, nor the next. As tempting as it was to hide in the darkness of her past and grief, she knew that the dark seduction to become one with the madness of the room's energy was not where she

30

belonged. She could feel its lure calling her deeper and deeper. She peered over at the open door of the closet, no longer completely darkened as the first day she and Layce opened it and broke through the wall. A small glint of light now exists from finding the room deeply buried behind the secret hallway with once covered windows, blocking the sunlight. Hidden in a strange maze of architecture and the thick ancient brush of trees and bushes up against its outside walls. She never knew it was there.

Hardwood shards of pointed wood shaved off and scattered on the floor of the closet from the time they kicked through the wall, wood rotting, to discover the sinister Cold Room that lay behind the closet wall, and down a lonely dark hall, hidden for years. Memory of that day and the plank of wood they found in the closet floor that was hidden and held hair with ribbons tied to it, and teeth; something that could have been innocuous, but alas, she found it was not. They knew a devious presence lingered, especially when it slammed the door shut and they could not get out. A child, a stain on a family wishing to hide what resided in that room and so was covered up. Murderous parents, if only to protect others, a murderous child, an evil child beyond imagination.

The child murderer had killed her parents and was fatally wounded in the process by the ones that brought her into the world after they discovered what she was; evil. No doubt they had found her Cold Room and were in horror. She remembered the discovery with disgust, the small, missing children cleverly dead and hanging on the walls for her, the girl, to view like a painting or take down to play with and pull more teeth from their mouths, or to sew them shut. The thought that she may have done this to them while alive haunted her nightmares. She could only pray they were already dead. Her heart ached for them.

Chapter Seven
Johannah

I have often wondered what causes someone to be this way. What demon parasitizes a joyous soul entering the world only to bury what was meant to be a kind person, so only a devil remains? It is unfathomable that a child could be evil. We just cannot see how something so soft and fragile at birth can become so demented, but the transformation does occur. We see it in our world every day, sadly, still, we cannot understand it. I don't understand it.

Life is so precious, she thought to herself. It is a gift we scarcely deserve, and yet we enjoy the bounty of God's grace with every breath. Even those who don't believe in a God, per se, understand the power of nature! *What a beautiful gift life is*, and as she had that thought, it was as if thunder struck in her heart and she felt a literal pain, because even her husband had taken it for granted when he killed himself. *What a fool he was*, her mind condemned, and she felt a twinge of anger at him. Not only for leaving her behind, but for taking life for granted. *What a stupid fool*, she thought angrily; the first time she felt any other emotion than grief and agony when she thought of him. She felt cold, she felt angry. She stepped beyond the shards

33

of splintered wood and crossed the threshold of the closet, into the Cold Room of death and began walking down its abandoned hall of hell. Her body screamed no, but she could not help herself.

34

Chapter Eight
Hell

The Cold Room could only be that Hell! The last final steps for so many children who had no idea of how deranged were the hands that held them and what monstrous things she would do to them. Jo tried to ignore her fear as she walked down the hall and into the Cold Room, the final hell of the lost children.

She felt a twinge of relief in remembering the apparition of those children and infants released from their jail, a recycling memory having gone on for what must have felt like an eternity, while the secret remained hidden.

She walked over to the window covered only slightly now by a white sheet, that allowed some light to break through. It still startled her, as she peeked out into the garden below, to know she had never seen or had any idea this room, this space, was here. How cleverly the family covered it with dense shrubbery and diversion.

Clearly they could not hide the news of the murders of the girls' parents and the girl, Ada, herself, who died from her injuries later. Only the story was reversed. The parents looked as though they had killed Ada; that they were the demented ones. But really, when Ada was found out by her parents, Ada killed them and then died from

35

their self-defensive response. History remembered the "poor girl, Ada". No one would ever suspect such evil of a child, especially in those times when women were considered so weak in frame and emotional disposition that they could never kill a man. That was partly how Lizzy Borden got off.

Women are not too feminine to wield an ax when they are being abused, or even if they aren't and just have motive.

But they did cover up the room so the greater stain on their family was not realized, at least in their lifetime. That stain being not only the family tragedy, but that a serial killer belonged to their family, the Purdy family.

That just could not happen. A family would not recover from such shame. They would have been shunned from society then; ruined. No, the family protected themselves as much as they could. A tragedy, society would forgive, a serial killer, they would not. The decision was made in haste to never disclose that room, and those little lost lives. The room was sealed, and the parents of the missing children would never know what happened to them. The extended Purdy patriarchs made a devastating choice for everyone. How do I know, since none of this was ever recorded, other than the family 'tragedy'? The Purdy ghosts themselves showed me against my will. And

36

see I did. They made me an honorary family member in a club I never wanted to be part of.

As she looked out, the landscape was cleverly created as a barrier, so one could never see the space of that room from the outside, protecting what was sealed in secret, inside.

She looked out and saw trees, Italian cypresses, hedgerows, soft touch holly bushes, red twig dog wood bushes all densely packed into the spaces between the house and the yard, while in a strange way, looking so perfectly placed and natural, free even. What she could not see from the room was that on the other side of all that brush was a small fountain, a steel arched garden arbor with wisteria hanging vines, and bougainvillea. Vines, ivy, lilac colored wisteria, purple and pink hydrangea bushes and coral and red colored geraniums, and so much green, wild-like plant life placed around, to distract the eye from realizing that the house had a room, hidden just beyond the secret shield of nature's bloom. You never once observe the house until you walked around the landscaping with all its glorious blooms of distraction where the eye is being directed to notice it. So clever.

It was so cleverly placed, and they knew that, over time, nature would secure their secret. And mother nature did not disappoint. Jo never, not even for one second,

37

stopped to notice that space in the house. Yet she already knew there was a master builder who understood how to deceive. She recognized that immediately when she saw how cleverly the closets were positioned in ways that gave more room inside than appeared from outside. It was magical. Only in this case, the savvy was directed for a darker purpose, and they were indeed successful.

The sleeping psycho (the girl) got bored with her hell, her abandoned hallway, her human souls she had been torturing for ages, trapped in time. She wanted to play with the new world and the people in it, and she locked her sights on me. I, after all, came right to her doorsteps. It's my home now, but she doesn't recognize that. To her, evil is forever, and she clearly enjoys the fear of others; seeing terror in people's eyes. She liked my sleepless nights, and me sleeping in the guest house to stay out of the monsters' way.

But as I think this thought, I think, *fuck her! I'm moving back into my house, and I may even do something really outrageous that I know she'll hate. I may just open this Cold Room and house up for stays and tours.*

The Purdy Murder House Tour & Stay

Maybe I will bring people in, to disturb her quiet secret and bring it into the light of day, taking away her power to hide in the shadows. And if she wants to play with people, then maybe she plays with a crowd that isn't easily scared, people who would be drawn to such a house, for fun!

This was a very intriguing thought; one she would give deep thought to and even ask some questions to Geraldine when she drove over to visit her to find out about making this house a true-blue historical site. Now it would be even more powerful if Purdy House, now known for the Cold Room, was literally on the map!

"Fuck You, Ada," Jo said aloud in her deep and calm voice, as she dropped the sheet down to the floor from the window and turned around and entered the abandoned hall, stepped passed cobwebs and spiders, crossed over the wooden shards on the floor, out of that demented world, out through the closet door, and out of the beautiful and sad room, into the house hallway, past all the rooms, velvet wallpaper, antique sconces and down the lavishly lined stairs, to leave, all the while tempting fate and knowing that little psycho would make her pay for what she just said, already feeling the dark evil building up in her home, following her out like a clingy shadow trying to consume her energy.

39

Sufani Weisman-Garza

They were locked in a battle and Jo never backed down from any battle. Secrets are bullshit from weak people pretending to be strong. *So, bring it, little bitch. Let's see what you got!*

Jo grabbed her purse, and walked out to go see Geraldine, making sure the dogs were safely lounging in the guest house, soaking up some lovely beams of light from the windows. She didn't trust that girl with her fur babies. And her fur babies were not as tough as she was.

She thought, *Maybe I should get a Doberman? Damian, that devil kid, had one. Maybe I need one to fight off a little devil? Lord knows Nos-Ferrah-Tu ain't gonna help me.* She giggled at the thought as she got into her car and drove out of her driveway.

The dark energy of the house vibrated with rage as she drove out of sight. A heavy film of darkness settled over the bones of the house, the luxurious gold and mahogany curtains, the rugs, the Victorian couches and chairs, the hard wood floors and decorations, the demilune, the candles, the candy dishes, the books. In an eerie silence, a sinister shadow heretic ran from room to room, furious and manic.

Furious! The dark shadow spread out!

Chapter Nine
The Office

She left the house and began to drive to the historical society to talk with Geraldine whom she had spoken to when she first got the house, a sweet woman with brown hair and curls, late sixties, who always wore funky cats' eyeglasses on a sparkly chain but found herself in a daze and taking turns here and there, winding up in front of Donovan's office. She put the car in park and gazed out the windscreen wondering how she got there and why her instincts took her straight to him? She wasn't there for therapy; she was there seeking his wisdom and support as a friend. She supposed it was a good thing that she thought of him as a calming balm to her agitated state. She was not there to dump on him either, she was surprised even by herself and the natural instinct to come to him when she felt this way. But he had proven his friendship to her through all the house turmoil and late-night calls in fear. Always, he was willing to be there for her and for all of her family in their time of need and fear.

Fiercely independent, she did not need a man to comfort her and keep her calm. What every person needed was a support system and, like it or not, Donovan had found the cracks in Jo and managed to get in. So here

41

she was, in front of his building and making her way into the lobby and then the office.

"Hello, Ms. Williams," Lucy, his assistant said. She was kind to not say Mrs. as it no longer pertained. She was a motherly sort of figure, pretty and soft spoken, yet you could sense a person who would take no prisoners if need be.

"Oh," Jo leaned in to say, "You can call me Jo, Lucy," and smiled.

Lucy, sitting at her desk leaned in to her as well and said, "I'm not supposed to, dear," with a whisper and a wink.

"Oh, I see," Jo responded with a wink of her own and the understanding between them.

"I don't see you on the schedule, dear, have we follied somehow?"

"Oh, no! I am here to say hello to my *friend* Donovan," she said annunciating the word, friend. And also wondering if 'follied' was actually a word. Either way, she liked it and was gonna use it.

Clearly, Dr. Donovan heard the dialogue and came out through his multi chambers of doors to his office.

"Ah, here he is, Ms. Williams. Dr, she's come to say hello," and Lucy put her head back down into her previous workload giving them the perception of privacy although

42

they remained standing before her desk. Lucy was a class act, all the way!

Donovan smiled at Jo, and she could have sworn his eyes twinkled, like in commercials. He was that good looking, dripping Keanu Reeves gorgeous vibes while having no idea how amazingly good looking he was. If he did, he never showed it or perhaps placed too much importance on it.

He was clearly happy to see her, it showed in his delight, the way you can see a sun coming up. You cannot hide the sunrise in someone's eyes, and he had it for her.

Jo was a bit more cautious with her feelings and also, with overcoming her past tragedy, taking her time with herself and her emotions to move on with her life.

"Come on back. I have a few minutes before my next client," and he turned back into his chamber hall and through the next doors into his absolutely beautiful office.

She always felt a sort of awe come over her when seeing his collection of furniture, so upscale yet serious, it screamed luxury that also was understated. So very much like Donovan. She loved the Robert Adam style chair, with a lovely teal tapestry and gold leaf. The entire room was full of the same style furniture, very elegant in style, yet comfortable. There was a matching loveseat, another chair with a black and teal pattern that was the Doctor's chair

43

next to a side table with the necessary tools for writing and such. No longer having her name etched in them. All soft lighting and antique style bulbs to create a feeling of comfort and warmth. If you were scared coming to therapy, it was not because of this room.

She glanced at the two-matching mahogany demilune commodes that were much like sofa tables, flush on one side to place against a wall or couch, stunning as the first time she saw them. One was against the wall in the entrance and one directly behind the loveseat.

The room had a darker teal color on the wall with mahogany-colored drapes with gold accents tying the whole room together. Each piece of furniture and decoration seemed carefully chosen for its uniqueness. Donovan was not only meticulous in his style, but in knowing who he was. He was a walking talking brochure of authenticity, sincerity and confidence, wrapped in humility. An amazing combination one does not get to witness often.

He sat on a chair and she across from him. Very different from their initial meeting.

"Want to have a bite to eat tonight?" Jo asked him, to the point.

"Yes, I do. Dinner, yes!" he also said to the point and emphasizing the word that she clearly didn't want to use making it sound like a date. A *dinner* date.

She smiled and looked down at her shoes for a minute and then up at him, out the window, and back at him again.

"Jo," he said as if scolding, saying, *give it to me.*

"I'm considering something outrageous, and I need to bounce it off you. You are a trusted advisor; a friend, and I trust you, like it or not."

"I accept, and I like it," he said with a smile, while standing up.

Jo took that as her sign to get out of his office so he could make money. She stood as well and began to walk to the door. He did not follow this time. He went behind his desk to find the journal and pen he was looking for and looked up. That he did not walk her out was a sign of friendship, as the professional in him would always walk her to the door. He did it on purpose to send that signal, and she liked it. It was silly, but they both were establishing to one another that they were now friends.

Although she only saw him a few times professionally and unconvinced she even wanted to be there, it always felt like they were meant to be friends, not doctor and patient, yet she could not complain as it was the thing that led her to him. It was also on the advice and harassment of her sister Layce and her mother, Lorna, that she get some help to talk out her grief. She really never did with him in the formal sense. They never got deep into it. The house fired up and took over her focus, perhaps even using grief to its advantage?

"Meet me at Dobbie's on 11th Street. I'll make a reservation, so we don't have to wait." Donovan looked up at her and smiled as she crossed through the first doors of his chamber and looked back, while standing in the hall.

"Six! I get hungry early," she said stopping and turning around to face him." You don't want to see me hangry," she said smiling and only half joking.

He nodded and laughed mildly under his breath to let her know he would take care of it and pushed the button to close the electric doors.

"Very 007," she said to herself walking out of the hall and smiling.

She wasn't in the mood for more heavy, cerebral topics of conversation today, other than the one she is going to have with Donovan tonight. So, she decided not to go to the Historical Society, and instead go to Mamma's Café and get a coffee and maybe a bite to eat, a salad or something light since she intended to eat good for dinner.

Jo loved tasty meals prepared by other people!

She drove, parked, and walked into Mamma's and was greeted by the ever so happy face of Ginni in true form as always yelling out her name.

"Jo, welcome in, sister."

Jo smiled and gave a wave knowing that Ginni already was making her memorized drink, Ginni's talent among many to know everyone's drink by heart. The "Sister" part of that welcome, being new, now that she is officially dating her sister Layce, while Rico, Ginni's ex, may or may not still be crying into his poodles over at the Doggy Transitional Spa and Happy Endings Rescue Shelter. Layce after all did steal Ginni right out from under him with no guilt at all. She laughed to herself and mused at the thought of her always sunshiny sister being a sociopath!

Chapter Ten
Gothic

She waited in her car, parked in front of the restaurant across the street. Of course, she did not know any restaurants really other than Mamma's Café because she had been a little busy ghost-busting her home unexpectedly, a job she would much rather not be doing, but she really had no choice. That beautiful gothic home was hers and with it came tenants she was unaware of until recently. Tenants that called out to her only, as all her previous research and conversation with Geraldine indicated no such issues until she moved in – none that were documented, anyway.

As she sat in her car waiting to see Donovan walk up, instead of awkwardly standing around waiting for him like a puppy, she saw Nina, the ice queen walk up. As though lightning strikes were coming out of the sky, she walked up the sidewalk slowly and assuredly, people just moving out of her way so as to not be struck down. From witnessing the reaction of the community to her, she wasn't well liked, or someone to be messed with either. The phrase, *scattered like roaches* came to mind, but not quite that bad.

Having been in her icy presence before at her own house, when Geraldine had an encounter with her at the Historic society around the same time that Jo's file had been out on the table while Geraldine did research. Nina inquired about the new owner. Geraldine kindly made the connection for the two to meet, so that Jo could gather more information on her property. Nina's family were direct descendants on her mother's side. Geraldine new Nina would be good for Jo to talk to. Nina had quickly informed her of her family lineage that owned the house, and so they were indirectly linked the way you don't want to be linked to someone. She was cold, perfectly put together in a gothic dark sort of way, but some might pass it off as professionally dressed in black, but it was more. She was sensitive, but for what side she worked was hard to tell. Like it or not, they were like forced family members you can't stand. And now they would be eating in the same restaurant.

"Great choice, Dr D," she said under her breath. She saw Donovan walking from the opposite side as Nina and they were on a collision course. She quickly jumped out of the car and walked calmy over to the target mark, the hostess desk, to protect Donovan from any potential unpleasantness.

As the two reached the host area at almost precisely the same time making eye contact, Jo stepped up the curb calling Donovan's name softly and ignoring Nina, who everyone could see and perhaps wished they couldn't.

"Oh, hello," Nina said tritely, as though bored by introductions. "If it isn't Ken and Barbie out for a morsel."

If there were any inkling that politeness would rule the day, that ended in seconds. The woman thrived off making people uncomfortable. She was an impeccably dressed junk yard dog. Dark eyeliner, blush and eye shadow, real night make-up, white as snow skin, eyes ice blue, wearing tight black skirt and accompanying fashion.

Donovan was of course blindsided as he had no time to see the whole crash coming as she did. Nina also had no time, but her native tongue was passive aggression and needed no advanced warning.

"Oh, hello, Nina," Jo said, moving her flowy strawberry-colored locks like a day at the beach, as she moved closer to Donovan, and they made friendly eye contact.

Turning to Nina again, she said, "Just back from the Goth convention, I see. And eating alone? How dreadful," Jo said pursing her lips and giving her a yoyo eye.

Nina smiled. She was clearly proud of her death metal looks and precision black skirts, four-inch heels she would gladly dig into your neck or eye socket if she had the chance. She had the warmth of a psychopath and Jo had no fear of her, which in a strange way, made them equals, and they understood it. They played with sarcasm and with perfection, like it was a ball at recess and Donovan's eyes were like someone watching a tennis match at Wembley.

Just as the words had come out of Jo's mouth a breathtaking six-foot man walked up to Nina who made eye contact with him casually and gestured to him in a wave looking at Jo, as a wordless introduction. The man was in a grey suit, dressed to perfection.

"Oh, don't worry about me, Josephine," Nina said, knowing her name was Johanna, not Josephine. Jo simply smiled, understanding the dig and thought it was funny. This whole thing was funny to her.

The man reached over to Nina, one arm touching her waist gently and affectionately, and looking at Jo, since Nina's daggers were directed there, as he put out his hand to shake Jo's.

Jo reached out to take it. "Lovely, to meet you," she said, "I loved your work in *Twilight*."

Donovan's head went down as one hand went nervously in his pocket, "Jo," he said under his breath almost as a warning she would want him to give to say, *be nice, be yourself.*

Nina had an evil grin like the joker.

"I'm sorry," Jo said shaking her head lightly and looking at the new gentleman's face that looked very set in powdered perfection and eyeliner. "I love the series *Twilight*, that's all. It was a compliment." She shook his hand, and he gave his name, which she didn't care about in that moment. She didn't want to be totally rude, though, so she was glad Donovan was there. It just came easy in Nina's presence.

Donovan checked them in, and the hostess came to deliver them to their table, leaving Nina and her gentle fellow in eyeliner to discuss the latest goth fashions and makeup techniques.

"So sad we cannot chat a little more," Nina said wickedly and smiled with evil perfection as they walked away.

Jo looked back as they began walking, Donovan in front, "No worries, Nina. I know you have to get back before sunrise."

"Jo," Donovan said quietly still looking forward, de-escalating things as they reached their table that would feel like a life raft.

Her comment, overheard by a few stimulated a dignified giggle, even Nina who seemed to revel in being frightful and disliked enjoyed the banter and attention from the community, even when it wasn't good!

Who needs to eat with such delicious passive aggression being served up? Jo thought to herself.

Chapter Eleven
The Table

"That was … interesting," Donovan murmured, pulling himself into the table and sitting comfortably.

"Hmm, yes, I worked up quite an appetite," Jo said with a slight laughter.

"I apologize Donovan, truly. I like to do my heavyweight boxing in the gym, but she likes it scrappy." Jo put her dinner napkin down on her lap and took a drink of water.

Donovan looked at her, not totally comfortable with what had just happened.

"In all seriousness, I am sorry that happened. Trust me, I had no idea I would see her. She came to my house once; her family lineage were one of three owners in its history to live in it. She came in like she owned the place, and she knew there was darkness there and seemed to know something but wasn't gonna tell me. Jerk!"

"Do you think she knew about the murders of the children and the truth about the parents and that they were not the guilty ones?" Donovan asked.

"She knew something, but honestly, it's really hard to say what evil lurks in her brain. Her resting face is *cunning delight* so it's really hard to read."

54

Taking a moment to look around she realized what a cool place they were sitting in.

"This place if amazing," she said looking around at the odd yet beautiful assortment of things hanging over head. Directly above them were seven glass lantern-like light fixtures in assorted shapes and sizes in different colors, pleasing to the eyes. Glassed cabinets on walls to the left and right that spanned the length of the dining area all filled with unique pieces that were enjoyable to look at due to their surprising, unique nature. She took a moment to realize what kind of place Dobbie's was.

"Yah, it really is," he said looking up and around, familiar with the magic of the restaurant.

"It's kind of … medieval meets comfort?" She said, not sure how to describe it. The lights were soothing, and the entire restaurant had a golden romantic glow. It was both casual and formal if you wanted it to be either. It could be fantasy or simply a place to get good food that sticks to your ribs. Jo was all in.

"That works," Donovan said and smiled. "And by the way, stop calling me Doctor Donovan. I'm not your doctor as you know.

They both smiled at each other and looked over the menu.

55

"Ooh," Wyvern Eggs for an appetizer. Deviled eggs, with gaufrette potatoes, and asparagus. She looked up and smiled with eyebrows raised.

"What's a Wyvern, and a gaufrette for that matter? Shucks, don't tell me, let's just get it!" he said with an adorably charming smile that lit up the room.

"You haven't had it before?"

"No, it's new. They change their appetizers often here to keep it fresh," he said.

For dinner Jo ordered the foraged mushroom steak with gravy, rice pilaf and garden vegetables.

Donovan ordered the roasted Cadboro Beast with twice baked potatoes, and carrots.

Although more exotic cocktails were available, they got some wine to relax and had no more run-ins with Nina, who seemed to be nowhere in sight. But just like a vampire, Jo felt her presence around!

"So, what did you want to talk to me about?" Donovan asked.

"I want to open a Bed and Breakfast. It will be called Purdy House. I will let people stay in the rooms especially advertising The Cold Room, for those horror junkies."

She had never seen Donovan's eyes so big, or seen him choke on wine before, until this very moment,

56

He wiped away his wine spittle and quietly looked around the room and back at her whispering and lowering his head. "Are you serious?"

Her response was simple.

"YES."

Donovan's eyes remained the size of black coals, staring at her speechless!

Chapter Twelve
The Discussion

"Jo," he said shaking his head in disbelief and worry. "Have you lost your mind?"

"I love this. I really do. We are definitely friends now cause you're a psych. doctor asking me if I've lost my mind," she laughed. "Just to assure you, no, I have not. Hear me out."

The food was served, and Jo looked at the entire display in amazement. Steam rising off their plates and the cutest little Wyvern deviled eggs you ever did see, the potatoes stuck on either side like wings with a very thin and yummy asparagus tail.

"Oh, so that's a wyvern," he said. "A tiny dragon of sorts," and looked up at Jo for approval.

Jo was already chewing the mushroom steak she had dipped into the gravy and then into the rice pilaf for the perfect bite.

"Oh my God, this is so good!" Jo said.

"Sorry little Wyvern," Donovan said talking to his egg as he bit into it. He picked up the tail and ate that too.

"Delicious," he said.

"Mmhuh," she agreed.

They smiled at one another very happy with their food.

"Ok, here is what I am thinking and why." She shoveled some vegetables into her mouth thinking of what she wanted to tell him first.

He quietly listened, non-judgmentally and with discernment. He was good at this.

"She is still there," she declared. Again, for the second time in one night, she saw his eyebrows rise and his eyes as big as coals.

"I thought she was gone," he said, concerned and devouring his twice baked potato.

"I went into the house, and, you know, I can feel her there. In my heart of hearts, I knew she was never really gone. She feels this is her home and I am a trespasser. I can feel her rage."

"So, you feel testing her is a good idea, Jo? I don't understand this."

"Listen, Donovan," she said changing her tone to one of seriousness and sincerity. "I have been through enough. This is my home," she said calmly, with a sense of belonging. "Maybe it's just my orneriness, but I am not going to be run out of my house. I came here to start over, and this weird situation is not going to make my life small and scary. I just won't allow it," she said, with more passion and a twinge of anger.

Donovan's hand reached out in a motion of pumping the brakes or, in essence, bring it down a notch, but at the same time was listening intently as a friend and beginning to understand her more.

"Why a bed and breakfast? Why bring others into what you know can be a very scary and even dangerous environment?" he asked.

"Because she wants to just torture me until I leave. But, if I open it up to other thrill seekers who are not afraid of such things, people who actually revel in it, they will not be so easily chased away, and essentially I am letting her do what she does, ad nauseum. They love being scared so it's not like I'm doing anything wrong to anyone. Full disclosure."

"Do you think that some of this is also that you feel by keeping her busy scaring others that she stays away from you?" he asked.

She chewed her food, and he took a bite. She bounced her head thinking that over as they both let the question linger while eating.

"I have to be truthful, yes, there is some of that. But I don't feel guilty about it because the people who will come here will have full disclosure of what could happen, what the experience is, and would definitely have to sign an iron clad waiver that I am not responsible or liable for anything that happens to them when here. I will get a lawyer for that because we both know shit could happen. Paranormal people love this shit," she said with a sort of whimsical tone and continued chewing.

Donovan also continued eating while not saying a word, even in the silent spaces. He was thinking, taking it all in.

After much silence and both of them finishing their meals, wine glasses long since remained empty, she asked him, "Well, what are your thoughts?" She knew that despite his personal feelings, he was trained to be logical, understanding everyone is different and must choose for themselves, and fair.

He finally spoke.

"I have a question, well, maybe a few."

"OK, let me have it," she said.

Just then the waitress came.

"I want dessert," she said looking at him and then the waitress. "I'll take the chocolate mousse, it's my favorite."

"Make that two pagan mousses," Donovan said cheerfully with a smile at her, and the waitress promptly left to get them.

61

"Where will you stay? In the guesthouse as you are now or in the house next to the Cold Room," he asked.

"In my room to be onsite," she answered.

"You feel okay with that being so close to the Cold Room? I wouldn't."

"No, not really, but I feel I will get desensitized to it if I do it. I refuse to let her drive me out. My room, by the way, has always been kind of off limits to her for some reason. Maybe her parents stayed there, and she remains out of that room. They were authority figures to her so that could be it? Anyway, I could change my mind but that's what I'm thinking. The guest house has three bedrooms and is a two story with a kitchen and a bath so, Mom and Layce will definitely stay there. Likely I will too when I come to think of it. Then I can rent my room out. That probably makes more sense. "

"Agreed. As far as the girl. psychologically that makes sense, despite the fact that she killed them later, but many children who have done this sort of things for a very long time obeyed their parents before … not!" he finished awkwardly, and they both laughed as the waitress brough their mousse.

"How will you handle your mother's visits, since she did have her own room in the house?" he asked with a very concerned look.

"Oh, that's easy. She will never sleep in that house again unless something drastic changes. I am going to prepare the old servants' quarters in the guesthouse into much nicer accommodation that will be just for family visits and my escape. I'll make sure that all the plumbing is in tip top shape for daily use and the kitchen as well for cooking. I imagine that there will be times when I don't want to be in the house and so I'll live there too. Now that we're talking all this out, it's more likely that I will actually make that my home and have family visits there. It will become my workspace also so I will be in there a lot, but haven't totally decided. I'm kind of playing that one by ear," she said casually.

"Ok, it sounds like you've really thought this out. Have you talked to Layce and your mom about this?" He gave her the stink eye.

She laughed with a snort, almost inhaling her mousse through the nose and coughed.

"No, not yet, but I intend too. This is a new chapter in my life, Donovan, and if this house is going to be such an anchor on me in the way that it demands, then why not have me lower the anchor and choose the terms. I actually think it could be quite fun."

Donovan smiled and asked, "What would you call it?"

"Mmm, maybe," she said thinking it over with her eyes looking up into her brain on the right: *"PURDY MURDER HOUSE STAY & TOURS"*

It was the second time she had gotten Donovan to choke in one night.

"Wow, I am really good at this," she said with no concern for his airways and in pure humor!

"You aren't serious … are you?" he asked.

"Yes, maybe. It's my first try at a title, I'm still mowing it over."

"Ok … keep mowing a bit." He said with laughter and they both giggled and bobbed their heads up and down in a yes.

They were actually having fun and it felt nice.

"Wait a minute," Donovan stopped. "Tours? As in, tours through the house?"

"Possibly, but more specifically, tours into the Cold Room," she said.

Donovan wiped his mouth and sat back as he let out an "Oh" and thought that over while looking directly at her.

"Yah! OH, is right! If she is ruining my quiet enjoyment, why not let me ruin hers," she said.

"Oh, I see, Jo. You are devious, aren't you?" he said laughing. "You may be a little twisted, too, but still charming!"

They both smiled. Donovan insisted on paying the bill, agreeing to let her pay next time.

It felt good to be happy again in that moment and hearing herself laugh again. Life was just beginning again, and she had choices. She wanted, no, *needed*, to make the right ones. Life was such a mystery that she allowed for the occasional mistakes she knew she would undoubtedly make in the future. What the hell. She had to take her pitch and swing, right? That's all anyone could do.

Swing!

Chapter Thirteen
Eyes of Darkness

She pulled into the driveway and drove slowly up as she looked at her house and stopped. She put the car in park and got out slowly. Standing by the side of the car, she looked up at the room on the right. She looked at the house, so beautiful, with such a stain it did not ask for her. Her native American roots tapping into the grounds calling her name, to be cleansed of the event it had no control over. The house was such a mix of beauty and sadness — like her own life, the parallels that brought them together perhaps; she and the house. She looked up again at the Cold Room, windows as black as night, devoid of any life inside., while the contrast of the remote smart timing in all the house cast the orange yellow glow of warmth shining out through its beautiful windows. She felt her watching and almost thought for a moment she saw a slight movement in the darkness in the Cold Room, but that could have just been her imagination. It was dark. Nonetheless, the girl was there, and her stain on the house always a blemish to her budding happiness.

She got back into the car that was still running in park and pulled toward the back servants' quarters apartments where she and the dogs would be staying for the night. She knew she had agitated the shadow of the house, and she was not up to engaging it further this evening. She had to give considerable thought to her idea, if she really wanted to start this B&B and tour, and what it would mean to her life, career, freedom, reputation; there were so many things to think about.

She also still needed to go to the Historical society to talk with Geraldine about the landmark and details of that for the home. She would do that in the morning to really understand what comes next and what the responsibilities would be and what support she would need.

JJo woke up refreshed and without incident in the cottage out back and with her trio of misfits snoring, grunting and farting.

"Nos, gross. You stink," she said as her sign to get out of bed. He looked up at her with a look like, "What? Smells like roses to me."

"We have to get ready to go see Geraldine today. I'll take you with me if you all agree to be happy and well behaved. Agreed?"

Ferrah yawned.

"That works for me!" and she got up, fed them first, put the coffee pot on and jumped in and out of the shower. She had her notes next to her as she got ready and looked over some of her ideas for the B&B, the tour aspect, and wondered if what she was doing was something she was sure of doing and each time, it rather excited her to know that she would increase this bond with her home in a whole new way.

Perhaps some would immediately want out of the home, but if anything, Jo felt an increased need to stay and work with the house. The current state of her not always sleeping in the home since the first major incident was only passing unless she decided to make the cottage a more permanent part of her path. She would take her time to decide. Regardless, it was her home, she loved it and was determined to find a way to live with history and not only that, but perhaps not hide from it. In many cases when these things happen, there is a shame attached to the home. But the land did not ask for this to happen. So much joy and love went into the home, the land, the gardens. The home was loved and filled with hope at the beginning. The stain of the past must not last forever on the home and perhaps she could help it heal, just as she was doing.

After she got ready she sashed up all the dogs and got them down the stairs and into the car for a joy ride. She hoped Geraldine wouldn't mind if they sat on the rather comfortable porch of the Historical Society when she went in to talk. It was like an old country porch wrapped around the old house, with nice comfy rocking chairs and décor to make it feel warm and inviting. The fur babies would be comfortable hanging out there in the nice, shaded area.

They all were in the car seats and off they went on their first family field trip to see Geraldine.

"Ok, kids, we're off to see Nana Geraldine," she said. "Hey, maybe Geraldine will like that she is called their Nana? I'll have to ask her permission about that," Jo said talking to them. "Remember, you all said you'd behavior."

Nos looked at her lovingly with "Anything for you, Momma," written in his eyes. She gave him little scratches and smiled as she pulled out of the driveway.

Chapter Fourteen
The Shadow of History

"Hello," Johannah called out, peeking through the cracked door of the beautiful old Historical Society building, rich with hardwood floors, beautiful wood working, rugs, books and even a staircase. She did not want to enter just yet, with the dogs.

Geraldine lifted her head and looked from behind her glasses, standing by a bookcase deep in reading and researching, yet always quick to smile to offer a friendly demeanor.

"Jo, come in," she said, looking at what Jo seemed to have behind her and why she was only peeking through the door, versus coming all the way in.

"I have my dogs. May they sit on the porch here?" she asked politely.

"Yes, of course, however, I just love dogs and as long as they are house trained to the calls of nature, well, they can come on in," she said sweetly.

Jo smiled and opened the door all the way revealing Nos, Ferrah and Tu in their harnesses with three leashes in her hand. Tu pushed his way passed his siblings and snorted his way over to Geraldine all on his own dragging his leash as he slowly made his way to her.

70

Geraldine had a crinkle of affection on her nose as she spoke to Tu and encouraged him to come on over and have a seat.

"Now, I just knew for some reason that you would be like this with animals." Jo said. "On the way over, I told them we were going to see Nana Geraldine, and I don't know why I said it."

At hearing that Geraldine's head snapped up in joy. "Oh, may I be their Nana? I would just love that! she said. "They are the sweetest little things. Come on, over here you two. Let Nana see you," she said to the others. Jo believed her to be the sweetest woman she knew in the city and just smiled seeing the love she was giving her little misfits and how much they were eating it up.

As Jo walked over to discuss business, the dogs knew to sit and make themselves comfortable on the rug by their feet, like good little fur babies.

"They are so well-behaved, Jo. You may bring them here anytime you need to." Geraldine said, reassuringly.

"Thank you so much, Geraldine," she said and began to get down to business.

"I would like to make my home a historic home on the national registry. I'd like to begin that process," she said, matter of fact but with a hint of insecurity.

71

Geraldine's face lit up. "Oh, Jo, that is so wonderful. I feel your home should have been listed long ago. In fact, it was nominated by our society. It is our job to seek out local areas we deem historical and make note of them for preservation."

"So, what happened?" Jo asked.

"Well, although it can be nominated by someone other than the owner, the owner can decide that even if approved, they do not want it listed. The last owners chose to not have it listed."

"That's odd. So, is it listed then, already?" Jo asked.

"No, they simply declined to have it listed. As the new owner, however, you can choose to lift that denial and move forward," Geraldine declared.

"Are you serious? That simple?"

"Well, quite a lot of work had already been done the first go around to get it approved. Even though the owners at that time declined to have it on the register, we continued our work documenting its value to the city, as is our job to do.

"So, they did not obviously pursue the registry themselves?" Jo Asked.

"No, others can request it if they see a historical value. The way it works, for example, is, you need a state preservation officer to nominate it, that is me. It went through me and a board to meet criteria. The original paperwork can be daunting, one hundred and fifty pages long and involve a letter of significance and must meet criteria, all of which your house has so much of. Each thing significant about your home is then researched historically to have the significance claimed, confirmed. As you know, your house was the first plotted in Gig Harbor, by Dr. Purdy, who was also the first dentist in the growing town and so it also produced revenue on the property. His home, your home, was also his place of business. You hear about people hanging their shingle out to work, well that literally was how it was back then."

"Oh, my goodness, isn't that something?" Jo said. Just then Nos snorted and they both looked down lovingly at him.

"They would have also been locally important as social development of the community. Doctors mean money, and money means high society. So, they influenced the town to be affluent. As you know, the physical property was documented as how it was then and how it is now. Local libraries keep all local history as well as even building materials for architectural accuracy. Isn't that amazing, Jo?" she asked rhetorically.

"Why the property is important to the town was also ascertained as the historical reference and function of

73

being the first home, first dentist, first architectural wonder, first social influencers, if you will," Geraldine said with a wink using today's terminology. "Now, here are some things you need to know. The listing is yours; I already know due to being approved prior. The federal government recognizes the listing as a federal planning tool, in essence, where to not build or plan and what is worth preserving. Although it is not a guarantee of safety of your property, it definitely secures it. Private locations can be preserved and even whole districts, as historical. Your home was approved through our Historical Preservation Society. We take care of all private listings locally. My grandson is a consultant for the States Historical Preservation Society and worked on it himself," and she gave Jo a wink.

"Wow, Geraldine, that was an amazing lesson right now and so fascinating. I can see why you love your job. So intriguing, history." she said with a smile and then drifted slightly into a faraway look. She looked down then to check on the dogs who were sleeping, except for Ferrah who was licking her toe nails. She was so precious.

Geraldine had been a model of class, having not mentioned once the trouble in the home. She knew Geraldine knew quite well what was discovered, and no doubt added that history to the records. It was official,

74

simple police records would prove it. There were bodies found and there's no hiding that from the record. History was history and must be recorded.

"Do you have a new purpose for the house, dear?" Geraldine asked curiously, looking down to catch Jo's eyes, her cats' eye glasses hanging at the end of her nose with her pearl chains holding them and dangling around her neck.

Jo smiled and looked around. There were just a few people around, still, she felt the need to whisper.

"You are obviously aware of what transpired in the home?"

Geraldine nodded without saying a word to allow her to finish.

"Well, I am dealing with that, and as you know from before the incident I was having paranormal occurrences in the home. This home is historical, listening to you, I do see now even more than I thought when coming here, that it has a significance to the town who may now really get to know it yet."

"Oh, I see," Geraldine said curiously. "You my dear have something up your sleeve I think I am going to be excited about. Do tell."

75

"Well, I want to open the main house as a B&B, preserve it in time, refurbish when it needs it to preserve it. Keep it frozen in time."

"And by the way there can be some tax incentives to do so, FYI," Geraldine informed her briefly, not wanting to interrupt more.

"I was also thinking of doing some tours of the Cold Room as well."

"The cold room, dear?"

"Oh, yes, you wouldn't know that term yet," Jo said.

Geraldine smiled; she was intrigued. "Go on."

"The Cold Room is the room that was found behind the closet. Behind the closet was a hallway that led to what we call the Cold Room, where all the children's bodies were found. Even the formal room housing the closet is part of the Cold Room. You can feel the cold the moment you open the door to the entrance. It's like a portal that does not match the energy of the rest of the house." She feared it may sound over dramatic but that was indeed the truth of that room in her house.

Geraldine put a hand to her lips, and her face got serious, "Oh, my, that's right. That is so scary. How are you managing with that? It must be somewhat scary to you, knowing that took place in your home?" she asked Jo.

76

"Yes, and no. It seems surreal in a way. The girl, Ada, her spirit anyway, is still there, I feel her presence and it is cold as ice, dark shadows ..." Jo trailed off.

Geraldine's eyebrows went up. "Well, you know, I will need to go over and see the room recently discovered for the review since we had not seen that space before."

"Yes, I hope you do come soon, and I will serve you tea and biscuits, too. But there is a hole in the closet. Will I need to do repair work before it can be approved?" Jo asked.

"No, that won't matter in the slightest and honestly, for what you're planning, I would say leave it exactly as the event found it, unfinished. It will add to people feeling what really happened there," Geraldine said insightfully.

"Thank you. That is a great suggestion. I will be interested to see what you sense. However, I want to also do tours through that space, while some of the other rooms will be used for a stay. I haven't yet decided if I will stay in the house myself in my room or remain in the cottage out back that has several rooms. Either way, I would run the property and also need to probably hire a chef so it will create revenue. I'm thinking that perhaps instead of hiding in shame, which was no doubt how the last owners felt and so did not want the attention on it

77

from a national registry listing, I would finally bring it out into the open, sharing all the history of it, which is quite important to the town. While people will know the tragic history, they will also learn their history and how and when the town was plotted and developed, etc. I'll also want to create a booklet in the home for others to sit and read the stories, in the sitting rooms where it all took place, while seeing historical pieces that have always been with the house as well as a written history. That is my idea anyway. Do you think that is crazy, Geraldine?"

"No, not at all darling. I want to be the first one to take the tour," she said smiling. "Now, I will send my grandson all the details you just listed and if he requires a formal letter of significance from you detailing more information, he will let me know. However, between him and me, I think we will get this through very quickly."

"How long does this normally take," Jo asked.

"Well, the filling out the forms is the longest, which is already done. Normally from the time the forms are submitted, we have forty-five days to process them and make a finding or make additional requests from the party requesting nomination. However, all that has been done as well. We are simply requesting the lifting of the denial of listing and giving the new details of how you intend to educate the town on its history, all of it!" she said with a smile and even a little pride. "What you're doing takes guts, Jo," she said, walking back to her desk. "I knew from the moment I met you that you had guts. I saw it burning in your eyes," she said, reassuringly. "I will be with you every step of the way and if you need any additional history for your books for the home and for guests, you come to me, and we'll put them all together. The Society has done so much research that we have pretty much everything you could ever need on your house, although you are telling us things about it we could never know," she said with a wink. "I am just so excited about this I can hardly stand it."

Jo smiled and roused the dogs and picked up their leashes.

"I'll call to schedule a visit to see the new room and also what you've done with the place so I will be prepared with any additional questions if I am asked by the board. Is this week or early next week okay?"

"Yes, Geraldine, any time, just let me know."

Geraldine politely walked them all to the door and she knelt down to Nos-Ferrah-Tu. "Now, you babies be good for your momma, and I will come by soon to say hello, and Nana will bring you some treats. Sound good?" she asked the dogs, looking each one in the eyes. Tu bumped Ferrah with his body to be in front to lick Geraldine's face and touch noses. Ferrah stood looking at

79

Geraldine curiously, while Nos kept his body facing her, but securely pressed against Jo's leg. He was loyal to Jo no matter what.

As they walked out to the car, Jo and her silly squad, she felt a quiet peace, like her life was taking a turn, one that she was in control of, and based on truth. She knew what she was entering into, she wasn't hiding in shame from her own life tragedy or that of her house. In a strange way, her life was paralleling the same lessons that both she and the house, must learn. Things happen in life we cannot control, and shame only deepens the secrecy and pain. She still did not understand why Clay took his own life, he was secretive to her about whatever it was that caused him to do it, and she was damn sure not going to hide from the town, from the house, or from her own life. So, heal they would do, together, no matter what it would take to get there. No matter what fierce opposition she faced with the unwanted tenant residing in the Cold Room.

As she headed home, she called Layce's number and put in her ear bud.

"Hey sis. Can you and Ginni come over for dinner tonight? I have something exciting to tell you both and I think I need your help to make it happen." After a few moments of silence in the car, with Layce chattering in excitement trying to guess what it was, Jo said goodbye and hung up. A smile crossed her face, as the wind whipped through her hair and for the first time in a while she felt peaceful and had a plan. She hoped the girls were on board for what she had planned. They were just the right women to pull off her shenanigans.

This could work, she thought to herself.

Chapter Fifteen
Ginni and Layce for Dinner

Ginni and Layce pulled up to the front of the house, the gravel crunching under the tires as they came to a stop just before the beautiful wide stairs that led to the wrap around porch. On command, everyone who walked up to the house couldn't refrain from looking up. The witch's cap and the two large windows upstairs pulling their eyes like magnets to look up and honor its magnificence, and if you knew the story, its horror.

"This house still blows me away. I mean, it also creeps me out a bit, but I love it as long as I stay away from that room," Ginni confided in Layce.

"Don't worry, honey. If anything happens, I am here and will save you."

Ginni laughed as a reaction she couldn't control. "Yah right! You couldn't even manage to get that fly out of the house. Talking to it and asking it to please leave," she scoffed affectionately. "And you're gonna protect me from a demented girl killer, or whatever else is in there besides dinner?" she said laughing and teasing Layce who knew she was right.

Layce wrapped her arm around Ginni's waist, and they climbed the stairs to the front door.

82

Bossa Nova was playing on the Alexa speaker and Jo was cooking up some delight that smelled amazing. The screen door was open. The porch was filled with monstrous sized ferns, rug runners in white, rocking chairs, side tables and a coffee table with potted geraniums blossoming. Everywhere you looked on the porch were places to sit and be comfortable with a book or some tea.

"Jo is doing a great job," Ginni commented. Layce nodded in agreement.

"My sister is good at anything she puts her mind to. It's a gift," Layce said as they made it in front of the screen door. Layce yelled out, "HELLO!"

Jo was in the kitchen, and they could see her through the living room. Her head popped up and she waved them in.

"Come in," she said busying herself with her creations. The dogs moseyed over to the girls as was their custom.

"Hey, Nos-Ferrah-Tu. How have you guys been doing? You look good," Layce said, kneeling next to them making sure to give them each an affectionate nuzzle and kiss on the head.

They looked at Ginni expectantly and she smiled and replied, "Hey kids, nice to see you again," and gave a nod of acknowledgement. When Layce was done giving them affection she walked through the living room to go see Jo in the kitchen and Ginni gave a quick pet to each of them and followed suit.

"Yo, what's for dinner, sis? It smells wonderful," Ginni said making a little sprint to catch up to Layce.

Meeting Jo in the kitchen with the smell of heaven steaming from a cast iron pan and the smell of warm biscuits in the oven, she said, "Oh, you are gonna be amazed and what I am gonna serve you tonight, and I'm not just talking about dinner." A deviously delicious and mischievous look playfully crossed her face as she poured the wine, food was served and eaten, and general love and affection sat at the table, with small morsels being handed secretly to three dogs who were under the table waiting for little bites at the apple.

The real conversation of what was to come would be their dessert!

Chapter Sixteen
Good Trouble

"OH MY GOD! Are you gonna tell us or what? I'm dying here," Layce yelled out playfully with a pleased and full belly, dying to know what Jo was up to.

Jo stilled herself in place at the table looking at her. She folded her hands together in front of her mouth, elbows on the table (much to the chagrin of her Victorian mannered mother who would slap her if she saw it).

"I'm gonna open the house up to the community."

The girls sat quietly letting what she said sink in and not really sure what that meant.

Jo was softening the information, perhaps not wanting a reaction quite like the one Donovan gave her. In that moment she realized she need not soften the language for anyone. She had made up her mind what she was going to do and that was her choice. But she did need the girls' help.

"Opening up the house…?" Layce said and trailed off confused.

"Instead of hiding the history of this house, I am going to bullhorn it by opening it up as a bed and breakfast and do tours of the Cold Room." She couldn't be more clear than that.

85

Eyes were round that she looked into; bodies frozen. It took three seconds to sink in before Lacye reacted.

"YAYAH!!!!! She yelled out cheerfully with a diphthong that would make anyone laugh! Her arms went up with fists, making a power gesture.

Jo's stiff back released; she lowered her head to Layce who sat across the table from her. "You're okay with this?" she asked and then looked curiously at Ginni.

"*Hell to the yah!,*" she replied. "This is *your* house. Trust me, sis, you aren't the only one who walks in a room and finds it hushed with little side whispers. People just don't know how to act with all the information about this house. So, if you can't beat 'em, join 'em," she said supportively.

Ginni looked at Layce and responded to her logic by nodding her head up and down in yes. "I agree," she chimed in. "The town *is* talking. As you know, the coffee girl hears everything. They try to dig info out of me like I know more or something. They think I am holding out, but they don't realize we are all just trying to figure out what the heck just happened and what to do about it."

Jo took a breath, realizing she had been holding it. She really did care what Layce and Ginni thought. These were her people and she needed good attitudes around her to help her define her mission.

Lacye saw her inhale a deep breath of relief. "Sis, we got you. We would support you no matter what hare-brained scheme you came up with. It's your life." And she reached out across the table, touching the top of Jo's hand.

Just then a large thump sounded, like a bowling ball had been dropped on the Cold Room floor. Simultaneously, Layce and Ginni's shoulders jumped, and Jo's head went up to the ceiling in the room across the formal dining room and into the front sitting room. They had heard that sound before. She was in there, listening and showing her disapproval. They all looked at each other.

In moments, Jo recovered, getting desensitized to the eerie entanglement with a killer ghost residing in her house.

"Exactly. This is why I am doing this. It's my house and I won't hide or be afraid of it," she said, as they all shook their heads, *afraid*! And she began to tell them her plans.

She continued on describing that there would be tours through the Cold Room, they would open the doors on a schedule, perhaps twice a day in the beginning. Jo would get a business license, draw up a legal consent and liability contract with each person who stayed, and tour

87

members would need to sign beforehand, as well as a no refund policy if anyone shag-asses out in the middle of the night or can't get through the tour. They need to know full disclosure what they are coming into and be willing participants in it.

She discussed with them that they would need to market in all the local spots and advertise with online paranormal communities. The target market are thrill seekers. Marketing was her jam, so she would do that research.

She would also run Facebook and Instagram ads for local outreach to announce what she was doing for the community. She would make an advertising video that would include the beauty and comfort of the Victorian home while mentioning the tragedy of it and the tour available. Perhaps she would have a special package that allowed those staying to pay a certain price for the detailed tour that allowed them to go into the Cold Room that would be off limits and perhaps rented out only once a month to a high bidder who could brave it. That would generate urgency and excitement. It would also attract paranormal researchers who would then post videos about it and create even more buzz. But it would remain a privileged thing to be in the room connected to the Cold Room behind the walls.

Layce interjected, "We could also invite certain special people who have huge followings to come for free and stay because they would be posting to all their YouTube following. This is the new age advertising. This is the sort of thing *Grimm Night Detective* loves doing, we could invite them for a free visit?" she said and looked at Jo.

Ginni chimed in, "Ooh, they would love that. I wonder if they would be brave enough to stay in the Cold Room?"

"I seriously doubt it, but that would be so cool to have them here," Layce said. "Jo, I'll send you a link to show you who they are."

"OK, that sounds exciting! You think they'd really come?" Jo asked.

"Hell yah! They live for this shit!" she said.

Jo continued and they listened with intent and felt the sensational excitement of her plan.

"It's so detailed," Layce said with surprise and awe.

"Yes," Jo said, amazed herself. "It's all coming to me so effortlessly. It's like every job and experience I have ever had prepared me for this and has put the right people in my life right now to make this a reality.

Ginni and Layce looked at one another as Jo continued on with her plan.

89

"I need you both to be part of it…"

"YES!" Layce blurt out! "This is so fucking awesome I can hardly stand it. Did you tell Mom? When will it open? Is Ginni gonna have a part? Will you stay in the home or out back? Oh, my God, I could never have imagined this!" Layce said, finally taking a breath.

Ginni laughed at the myriad questions that just came out of Layce's mouth. Jo was accustomed to it.
"Slow down, tiger," Jo motioned with her hands pumping false brakes. "Here is what I need," she said, leaning in. "Layce, I need you to do the tours and help me with the responsibility of checking people in. I will manage the bookings, booking for the normal rooms daily and Cold Room stay once month, advertising and also linen turn over. For now, we will do it but if we get really busy we can hire a cleaning service to do pick-ups and delivery. That's the ultimate goal. If we start and it becomes booked immediately, we'll revert right to that plan. If its onsie-twosie we can manage ourselves. Ginni, I know you love to cook and do coffee magic. I know you don't get to do much cookery over at Mamma's, so, if you want to do a little more here, you can. We will provide a continental plus type breakfast to every person the morning of their stay with some sort of scramble or frittata, versus just a boiled egg, which I always hate when I have stayed

90

somewhere. Not everyone likes hard boiled eggs. So, a simple scramble or frittata with peppers, mushroom and spinach every morning, with croissants or pastries, and local fruit, coffee, tea, juice, water. We could cater it from Mamma's, but I wanted to give you the opportunity to perhaps come in the morning here before you head to the café as we get started. You could be the chef of the B&B and I would put you in control to make sure all foods are ready each day. But that also means, not too much, not too little. Just what we need per our bookings. We would work together on that at first to make sure it's just right. Since we don't know how it all will go yet, I wouldn't want you to make any drastic changes to your schedule at Mamma's Café until we see how it goes. And really you would never need to change anything if you wanted to be here and there. That is, if you want to be part of this which, OMG, I am just going on like I know you want to do it. Ginni, I'm so sorry. Please don't feel pressured," Jo said and reached out to touch her shoulder sincerely.

Ginni laughed, "Are you fucking kidding me, dude, of course I want to do it. This is the most exciting thing that has happened around here for, well, since the last time here, with the bodies...and the teeth... thangy," and she turned her head like the exorcist girl, referencing the other room where a portal of teeth bombarded the room

91

incredibly, pouring from the ceiling, coming from the Cold Room, defying logic, and science.

Jo let out a sigh of relief and leaned back in her chair.

"Seriously, how long have you been planning all these details Jo?" Layce asked.

"A lot of them literally just came out right now. I think I finally gave myself permission to put it all out on the table. I think I was waiting for the right audience to spill the beans to. Thank you, both," she said looking at both of them in the eyes, "for being so supportive."

"This fricken rocks," Ginni said, looking at Layce and then looking back at Jo with a huge smile.

"Do I quit my job, Jo?" Layce asked. She loved exciting changes.

"Sister, hang on to it right now as we are putting this together. Just like Ginni, let's move steadily and not urgently. We have a plan, and we can start to move on it. I was actually even thinking that if you wanted to, sis, you could offer massage to the people here, or we could make some sort of deal with the spa. Although," she thought, "it would be more lucrative for you to do it here. We could create a space, maybe even build a special room or even just a beautiful yurt style building on property if you want to keep doing it. It could be called, *A Spa Massage Just for Yurt!*" Jo said, laughing.

"I LOVE that," Layce said laughing with her sister. "Yah, let's do that. That way we can adjust at any time based on what we need for the business, and we have control of the schedule and the money. Also, I have connections with the other massage therapists that…"

Jo cut her off. "We would just place an ad, I don't want any local businesses mad at us, but you can still tell your close people on the DL, but I would have plausible deniability that we didn't steal any therapists. I could just say I placed an ad, which I would. Actually, if you wanted to refer any people, I would just have you have them apply as usual with your reference. We would need someone on stand by for when you are off or need a break, or actually, we may need two people for different shifts anyway." Jo said. "However, top priority is getting all the other details in order: Licensing, much more bedding to change out, fresh towels, soaps and that sort of thing. I can make a list. Ginni, you know a lot of people, If I make a list could you refer locals to me to buy from and also do the jobs, like build a yurt?" she asked and smiled. Just saying the word 'yurt' made her smile.

"Yes, of course. I know everyone and surprisingly, my uncle's best friend is a builder and also has built many yurts, believe it or not." Ginni said. "It's a Pacific Northwest thing," she said, realizing it was quite amazing to be in need of a yurt, and know someone who builds yurts!

"Wow, thank you so much. I will put that list together tomorrow and have it for you this week. Tomorrow I will be buying all the bedding and stuff. The rooms are already gorgeous," she said.

"Anyway, I have to do my part before it all goes live and before either of you are affected. I will keep you posted daily of where I am in the process. To be honest, it's selfish on my part because I am nervous and will second guess myself often on this so having you there talking to me will make this more real and reassuring," Jo admitted.

"We got you," Ginni and Layce both said. Then turned to one another and smiled while holding their hands by the side of the table.

Jo smiled lovingly at them. "Also, I am having the home put on the National Historic Registry. I forgot to mention that yet," she exclaimed.

Layce let out her excitement "That's amazing!"

"I know, and apparently the society tried to have it listed already so all the work was already done to make it happen, all the history documented, and the value of the home to the city for historical reasons. Forms were done so I don't have to prove any of the things I would have to help them see why this home is a value to the city."

"So why didn't it happen then," Ginni asked with a furrowed brow.

"Apparently the owners at the time can choose not to list it, which the last home owners chose not to for some reason. I think maybe they knew something was up with this house and didn't want to draw any more attention to it."

"Hmm, that's interesting," Lacye pondered.

"Right," Jo said responding with eyebrows lifted. From talking to Donovan who grew up with the boys in this house, he said they never had any problems. Now I think maybe they did and suffered in silence. I mean, it is possible that the spirit was dormant, but the fact they declined a historical listing seems strange to me. Especially because it came with certain tax perks, and no doubt the sale of the home would have been even more lucrative with a historical significance, I would think anyway, but what do I know?" Jo got up and began clearing the table. The light over the table flickered. They all looked up for two seconds before resuming.

"How long will that take?" Ginni asked, as they also got up and helped her put away dishes in the dishwasher, clear the table and put leftovers away. Ferrah started to whine under the table which was not like her.

They all looked back at them under the table. The dogs didn't come out as they normally do.

"Uh, oh," Layce said.

They all began to hear a low vibrating sound of humming that grew in intensity. They were all hushed into confusion. Suddenly, the single wine glass left on the table exploded! The dogs bolted to the library instantly like a greased fart on a lightning rod.

They all covered their eyes in reaction and then looked at what had happened. Little red wine droplets covered the white table cloth like blood splatter.

They stood in seconds of silence.

"Ooh, we are gonna sell so many tickets," Layce said, terrified and so excited!

Chapter Seventeen
The Society Visit

Days had passed and the weekend had come and gone without incident. On Monday morning, Jo got a call from Geraldine to schedule the home visit to review the Cold Room, the part that was hidden from all observing eyes on her last visit before Jo owned the home. She agreed and scheduled it for Tuesday; today. No need in stalling it. She was wondering how Geraldine felt about coming to the house, and knowing what she was about to see, that is, knowing the history now.

The doorbell rang and the dogs rushed from the library, their favorite hangout, which was to the right of the front door, from the inside. They ran snorting and barking as they always did when someone knocked, or the mailman came. They looked at Jo for approval. They wanted her to know they were protecting her. They weren't quite the guard dogs she had been looking for when she went to the Ruff Times and Happy Endings _Transitional Dog Spa, but they did the job. They had let her know every time something was amiss in the house and that was a form of protection.

97

She smiled at them and gave them all a loving scratch before opening the door. She could see through the glass widows of the door who stood in front of them.

"Geraldine," Jo said opening the door with a cheerful welcome. "So happy to have you here with me as the new owner. Yay!!!" she said.

Geraldine gave Jo a hug, which Jo was surprised by, but also welcomed, and soon after that Geraldine began talking to Nos-Ferrah-Tu. "Hello my little grand babies. Nana said she would bring you treats when I came to your house, and Nana always keeps her promise. As she said that, she pulled out a treat bag from her purse and quickly looked over at Jo for permission.

"May I?" she said with raised eyebrows. Geraldine was the cutest older woman, her mother's age, she though. Cat's eye glasses on a pearl chain, flowy clothes reeking casual beach class and a gentle, peace like demeanor. She was possibly the sweetest woman she had known in Gig Harbor.

Geraldine kneeled down and absorbed the love and kisses from the misfits and handed them each a small dog treat, making sure they ate every last bite. Once they did, she pulled out one more chew treat, and they took them and headed back into the library to take the task of

98

demolishing their dog treat seriously. These would take time. She stood up.

"Want some tea?" Jo asked, to be polite.

Geraldine looked up at the ceiling to her right as she faced inside the home. "The room is above, there, right?" she asked, in a serious and quiet tone.

"Yes," Jo said, in all seriousness.

"Perhaps we do that first, and then sit to have tea. I will confess, I am a bit…nervous for some reason. But at the same time," she said, with ghoulish delight, "I am also somewhat excited. Is that terrible?" she asked.

"No, not at all," Jo said, understanding. In fact, that was exactly what she was thinking all others would feel coming here when it was open. Curious, nervous, perhaps a little terrified and thrill seeking, also those who want a beautiful B&B experience in a Victorian home.

"Let's set your things down in the library, it seems to be a safe room," Jo said, and just then she saw a micro expression in Geraldine's face shift to one she could call, fear. It was only there for a moment, but she saw it. "Look, Geraldine. I know this is your job and all, but I have to tell you now, I can't promise nothing weird won't happen. I hope not, but I can't promise it. I need you to acknowledge that before we go up."

Her face flushed. "I acknowledge it," she said, feeling a little creeped out.

"Nothing has happened in the last few days since the glass incident, so we should be fine," she said as she began walking up the front steps to the second floor. There were also back stairs leading to the same landing. It was the one she used more often. They would have been the servants' stairs.

"Oh, goodness, Jo, that only means another incident is looming." She stopped at the first step, closed her eyes, said a little prayer in silence and did the sign of the cross. Jo simply looked back and smiled at her. *If only that was what it took*, she thought to herself. She waited for Geraldine to be ready before she resumed climbing up the stairs to the top.

At the top of the stairs, they made a U-turn to face the long hallway. The antique wall gas light sconces flickered like candles do naturally and the opulence of the hallways were breathtaking. In the evenings Jo would light them one by one in a sort of ritual she enjoyed doing down a long hallway stretched out toward the front of the house, two rooms on the right, and one on the left at the end of the hall.

"Is that it?" Geraldine asked in a whisper, looking at the last room on the left toward the front of the house.

"Yep, that's it," she said casually. Jo had developed the sort of morose humor or even desensitization one would get in the circumstance of living with something terrifying from day-to-day.

Geraldine looked around. "It's still the same but renewed, somehow. Jo, I think the house likes you," she said.

She looked around and took in the rich mahogany of the hardwood floors, lined with rich, expensive rugs for the expanse of the hallway, colors of mauve and gold, velvet wallpaper, perfectly placed tables with flowers with dim lights so there was never a moment the hallway would be dark, at any hour.

"You burn the gas lights in the day?" Geraldine inquired.

"Only for your visit," she smiled.

"Oh, isn't that sweet," she said still whispering and then got serious again as she looked back at the Cold Room door.

"Are you ready to take a look, Geraldine?"

"Yes," she said, not sure at all, and they began walking. Then Geraldine touched Jo's arm stopping her. "Before we do, tell me what is — tell me what I might experience, so I am ready for it." She was clearly a little scared, it was obvious now.

101

Jo turned around, her back to the Cold Room, and told her, "It will feel colder than out here. You may even see your breath at some point. You could have your hair pulled or be thrown. Things could explode around you or fling across the room. It's all possible. But we are together, and we'll have a quick look, so you can get what you need to satisfy the society forms. Deal?"

"Deal," she said scared and peering into Jo's eyes and then forward. Jo walked forward, Geraldine continued to hold her shirt at the arm and when they reached the door Jo opened it with the skeleton key. It creaked as it opened. The room was completely black, like a portal's mouth.

"Oh dear," Geraldine said from the hallway, already, cold breath coming from her mouth.

"Yep, 'Oh dear' is right," Jo said, and they crossed the threshold into the Cold Room.

Chapter Eighteen
Oh Dear

Jo turned on the light switch that she had to step into the dark room to do. As always, the light would not turn on. Many times, before she would have to go directly to the lamp and turn the bulb tightly to get the light on. Every single time, the light continued to be unscrewed, which of course, was not a *natural* occurrence.

The light went on, but the room had its own ambiance.

"The room is beautiful Jo; you have done amazing things to the house. But…" she said pondering, "What is this haze in here? It feels, like, well, as if we are in a dream."

"Yes, I would say more like, we are back in time, or in a nightmare."

Geraldine's eyes got big; that was it. "Yes," she said still whispering and intrigued. "I see the new, antique items, but it feels like we are… not in this time," she said amazed.

"Take a look around Geraldine and see the bathroom and other items, look out the window, before we head in."

Jo supervised this little field trip and was acutely aware of energy shifts that Geraldine might not be aware of yet. She felt responsible for this lovely lady and was very observant.

Geraldine walked to the window, looked and smiled at the ceiling and the crown molding, the wallpaper, the end table and all the small touches Jo made to make it feel authentic, using only period pieces.

"Jo, you have done VERY well." She looked at the bedding and then walked over to the bathroom and took in every inch of the room. The architecture was superb and now with Jo's attention to details and feminine touch, it was spectacular. She then turned to Jo and nodded.

Jo nodded back and walked toward the closet, when she opened the door to the closet, a beam of light came from within, from the Cold Room which lay in the back. The opened wall, looking very much as it had the day it was busted open, lay there for her to see. No attempt had been made to fix it, and none would be, moving forward. Cataloguing the day it was torn open seemed important.

"Oh, my," was all that escaped her lips. Jo opened the door all the way to the closet and leaned down to secure it to the stop, something she did shortly after the door had been slammed on her and Layce locking them in the closet. Now, there was a secure latch that was screwed into the wall that kept that from happening. Geraldine understood that instantly without asking a question.

Jo then turned on the center light with the string chain pully and entered. She looked back at Geraldine who hadn't moved an inch closer. Jo had to laugh.

"Come now," she said and waved her in. Jo turned and stepped over the wall into the once secret hallway. Geraldine followed suit. The alternative was she was standing alone in the front room, which although beautiful, she knew was not right. Geraldine entered the closet and stepped over and into the second creepy threshold of the day. They were now in the secret hallway.

Like church, they remained silent. Not a word was spoken. The weight of what this room was the same for every person who came in. For the children who were murdered here, this was their final walk of their life. It was hard not to be silent in the presence of that thought. It was difficult not to feel a deep sense of sadness and dread.

Geraldine looked at the hall, touching the wall and studying the original wallpaper that was more stately than that of the house outside this chamber and in shades of cream and browns. It peeled with age and led to a very creepy ambiance, as peeling wallpaper always did anywhere it could be seen. The hardwood floor was not cared for and aged poorly with time, looking dry and

105

weathered. Jo led her back the Cold Room where the discovery was made. She froze with one foot in front of the door, afraid of what she might see.

"There is nothing more here to see, Geraldine. They're all gone," she said, referring to the children they found hanging as corpse dolls on the walls. Geraldine's eyes closed as though blocking out what Jo had just said, it was too horrible to think of.

Geraldine stepped into the third hellish threshold and although the children were no longer on the wall, their outline was, and she was overcome with emotion. The stain of death was still present, on the walls, and in the way the room oppressed its occupant. Badness had scared this room. "Oh no, no, no," she said, her eyes instantly welled up as she looked upon the outlines.

Jo simply said quietly, "Look quickly, get what you need." She looked up at the ceiling, drying her eyes and recovering her senses, looked around at the wall paper and floors, noticing they were much the same as the hallways as expected, the desk in the center of the room where deadly deeds were done. She could take no more and her flight response kicked in. She turned and moved faster than Jo had seen an old lady move, her short heels clacking all the way. She hadn't even looked to see if Jo was behind her, but she was. Geraldine was Geraldine!

Gerladine was now in the hallway in front of the Cold Room door and felt safer standing there. She faced Jo waiting for the closet door to be unlatched and shut behind her. Somehow, Jo felt much better closing that part of the house behind a door, and then another one. She turned out the light, stepped out of the room and locked it with the same skeleton key. Jo was steady and precise. She turned to face Geraldine who's eyes were as big as silver dollars. Jo said nothing. She simply locked arms with Gerladine and slowly walked to the back staircase that led to the kitchen down stairs.

When they reached the bottom of the stairs and inside the kitchen Jo noticed she was shaking.

"Let's have tea in the cottage," Jo said, knowing she did not want to be in the home any longer than she needed to now. "I'll get your purse and the dogs." Jo walked over to the library in the front of the house, only to find Geraldine on her heels. She smiled, comfortingly knowing how afraid Geraldine really was.

"Nos-Ferrah-Tu," she said, and they all looked up, still happily chewing their treat from Nana. She grabbed Geraldine's purse and handed it to her.

"Let's go have tea with Nana in the cottage." They dogs all got up and they all walked down the long hardwood hallway, lined with expensive, beautiful rugs,

107

gold and mahogany colors, velvet opulent wallpaper, a long bookshelf filled with books, a demilune table with an amber nightlight and vase of flowers, to the back door, exiting the house, down the stairs and into the cottage to have tea and de-traumatize Geraldine who clearly misunderstood the power of the situation. Poor thing. Nothing that tea wouldn't set right, well, kind of! She had Donovan on speed dial if Geraldine needed a therapy session after her visit. Her fear was palpable.

It wasn't funny, but all Jo could do was acknowledge it and the more the terror energy filled the house and others, the more normal it became to her. She knew … it wasn't.

When they entered the cottage the feeling was entirely different. It was a cottage home, soft, bright, lots of soft white, like living in a big pillow. She asked Geraldine to sit and pulled out her chair, took her purse and sat it on the counter and began to boil the water. She put out the cups and made a small plate of scones and sat with her waiting for the water to boil. Her eyes, still saucers. All she could muster was,

"Oh, dear!" Her eyes were glazed.

Chapter Nineteen
Meant to Be

"Geraldine was terrified," Jo said. "Is this insane what we are going to do?"

Jo and Layce sat in the cottage discussing it in the little comfortable sitting room with simple floral print wallpaper on the walls in white, cream, pale pinks, forest green and splashes of gold. Jo had placed fresh cut hydrangea flowers in round glass bowls on a few tables in the guest house that made it feel homey and even sweet. Colors of pinks and greens did much to light up the room. "Heck, no, you know these paranormal folks love being scared, They live for this shit," Layce admonished. "But for some of the regulars who think they can brave it, make sure that it's clear in the paperwork that there are no refunds. I think we should also state that clearly as we hand them the key. Also, that's kind of cheeky! Don't you think?" Layce smiled at Jo who nodded yes and smiled.

"Well, I did actually give a tour of the Cold Room, and I learned what to say, so, I sort of have an authentic script of what to say to people before entering. Geraldine stopped me on the way to the door and asked me what to be prepared for. So, I will add that in to each tour. I

109

actually wrote it out that day, what I said to her, so we all have it," Jo said.

"And what did she say about it."

"Her flight response kicked in in the Cold Room, she cried when she saw the stains on the walls. She wanted out of the house, so I served her tea in the cottage but honestly, I could tell that she wanted to go home. She was traumatized. I think in the script I should add that some have felt traumatized from the remnants of the crime left behind in time. I didn't mean that to rhyme, *remnants of the crime, left behind in time*," she said playfully, "but whatever, you know what I mean?" Jo said.

"How about I stop over there tomorrow and bring her some flowers, something cheerful to make sure she is okay. I will say it is from us."

"Layce, that would be perfect. Thank you. That is a wonderful thought,": Jo said. As she was pouring them tea, Ginni came in, no knock. No need, it was just them.

"Tea?" Jo asked her.

"Oh, no, thanks," she said and kissed Layce and sat down. "What did I miss?"

"Geraldine was traumatized and cried."

"She did?" Ginni said surprised. "Wow, that's crazy. Is she okay?"

"Layce is gonna go bring her some flowers from 'Us' tomorrow to check in on her, make sure she is okay. It is a spooky thing to see."

"No doubt," Ginni said. "Okay, I have news. First, Here is a card for a lawyer to draw up papers for your liability waver. My Gran said her family has used him in business and he is reputable. Drop the Macpherson name, and he will know you are a special referral." She handed Jo the card, as Jo sat to drink her tea. Jo placed a cloth napkin on her crossed knee. "Next, my uncle who knows a guy who builds yurts and other stuff. I talked to him in the coffee shop today."

"You did?" Layce asked enthusiastic.

Ginni's eyes lit up at Layce with similar enthusiasm.

"Go on," Jo interrupted.

"Oh, yah," Ginni said looking back to Jo. "So, the smallest yurt is a little over one hundred square feet. Perfect for what you are planning for it. Normally it costs about 7.5K or so, (Layce's gasp was ignored), but he is willing to do it for you, at the Macpherson discount; 5K. He said he had leftover supplies that actually allow him to lower the cost. Another job let him have the leftover lumber and parts so he can use it for your project. If you want that done, here is his number. He is expecting your call, use the Macpherson name."

111

"Ginni, your family aren't like, Mafia or something are they, all this Macpherson stuff," and Jo laughed.

Ginni laughed. "No, we just have family money, old money, and have been in this town forever so we know everyone from cooks to lawyers and builders."

"One more thing," she said. "He was going to be on vacation next week, but said he would rather work, so he can start next week, and it will be done in one week. He can start this coming weekend and be done by next. Up to you."

"Wow, that's amazing. Yes, let's do it," Jo said excitedly.

"Great, I'll text him to let him know and tell him to expect a call from you to work out details and touch base."

Jo nodded and looked at his card with a smirk. She was happy this was rolling along. Only things *meant to be* rolled out like this. Out of all things meant to be, she thought … What a strange life!

"Also," Layce said, "I was in the café waiting for Ginni to get off and noticed a girl in spa attire. I asked her what she did, and she told me she was a private masseuse. I told her about an old home about to open up as a B&B, no other details, and that the back of the property would have a building built for spa services. It would be part-time, flexible, when we were ready, the off schedule to me, and

112

if it sounded like something she would want to do to supplement her income? She was interested, sis. So, we have a backup person. I kind of pre-interviewed her already. She went to East West Natural Institute for Massage and Natural Medicine, has 840 hours, more than necessary, well versed in many styles and perfect to represent us and our business."

Ginni and Jo blinked like South Park characters.

"What?" Layce said.

"Layce," Jo said. "I think we just saw you all grown up. You sounded like a boss, bitch!" Jo said laughing. "You're hired!"

They all chuckled.

"Layce, Spa Manager and Guest Tours. Ginni, Catering Manager, and me, Caretaker, Stays and Tours." She looked around at them all and saw nothing but happy faces in agreement. "Ok, this is exciting," Jo admitted.

"I do want to talk to you about menu and schedule for guest meals, to start thinking about how I will manage it and my time. But I'm hungry, can I make a sandwich or something first?" Ginni asked.

"Of course," and Jo waved her off into the kitchen. "Anything," she yelled out. They would spend the rest of the night talking about things and the next day she would begin setting appointments and making calls to lock things

113

in. Ginni was a lifesaver, and she thought maybe she should start calling her the Godfather.

Layce happily was eating a scone and noticing the condition of her nails.

Chapter Twenty
The Passing of Time

Just as Layce told Jo in the guesthouse during their talk, Layce checked in on Geraldine, and she was fine. That woman is tough and snapped back right away and was more excited than ever for Jo to start the *Purdy House Stay & Tour*. She had felt that the official historical registry would be affirmed any day.

Jo had been in her own little world with the dogs, shopping for more linens and pillows to switch out regularly. She had found the previous upstairs servants' area where the linen closets were, and where the laundry shoot was (that she never used personally), was now going to be used again by a servant; her, caring for the guests and having all the right amenities available to make it a nice stay. There were three rooms upstairs and two below with a restroom. All the upstairs rooms had their own ensuite, which was a fancy way to say they each had their own bathroom.

She carefully stocked all the towels in three sizes: face towel, hand towel, bath towel, beautiful bath salts to be used in the bathroom for luxurious soaks, enough to have a new one at each turn. She had decided against single coffee pod machines for each room since she would serve coffee and tea in the dining area all day long for the guests to come down at any time they liked and really enjoy the house. She decided to also have large antique glass cake holders with heavy glass lids to hold scones, croissants, and cookies all day long. She wanted to encourage the guests to come out of their rooms and sit in the old historic home, have some coffee or tea with a treat and perhaps read a book from the library, or take a look at any of the old relics from the home that she had placed meticulously and beautifully all over the house to really show its place in time. She hoped that all the guests would see how special the home was, even with the tragedy. Home was more than tragedy and she wanted people to get a taste of that fact.

She had been decorating all day and putting things where they needed to be as though strangers were coming. It needed to feel like a B&B, and that meant she needed to be professional.

The landline phone rang.

She walked from the servants' work station upstairs by the back staircase and walked to her room turning right, into her room, and away from the Cold Room.

"Hello."

"Hey, Jo, it's Donovan."

She laughed, "You know, you don't have to say that every time you call. I actually know your voice and name now," she said playfully and chuckled.

He laughed, "Oh, okay, good!" he said. "Just checking in on ya and was wondering how things are going? I saw Ginni at the coffee shop today and she said your plans are full speed ahead."

"Ah, yes, Ginni. That girl is amazing. Did you know she knows absolutely everyone? If you ever need something, she can get it for you, and at a discount. It's pretty cool knowing someone so resourceful," she said, almost to herself.

"I have heard that about her, actually," he said. "Anyway, heading home from work. Possible to stop by and say hello?" he said confidently.

"Sure, I could use the company and I would LOVE to show you what I have done so far."

"Ok, that sounds great. Do you need anything before I come over? I can stop on the way if you do."

"No, I'm good, thank you though. Come on over," she said playfully.

"Ok, be there in about ten minutes."

They hung up and she remembered a large table she would ask him to help her bring up from the basement that could be used for the check-in desk. She thought it needed to look more professional than just doing it at the kitchen island or table.

"Hey Donovan. Come on in," she said and opened the large front door, and the dogs greeted him as warmly as she did. He looked up at the ceiling and around at all the walls, furniture taking in the whole house. He did it every time naturally, but not because of the story of the house, but more for how much he appreciated it. He had seen it as a boy and had a special connection with it from having friends who lived in it when he was young. So, he was no stranger to the house, but never heard a peep about anything paranormal from his friends.

"Are you hungry? I can make sandwiches?"

"That would be nice," he said, "but first, show me what you have been doing in here. It feels different. More homey. Something has changed."

"I have been decorating and using pieces from the basement since they came with the home. I thought it would create more intrigue for people to see actual pieces that have been with the house as long as the house has been alive." She smiled.

"Interesting choice of words," he said mischievously, with a smirk. "But yes, I definitely think that is a great idea to add to the home. And it has become more alive, as you

118

say, filled in with more atmosphere of warmth. And the basement, ooh, shiver me timbers!" he said. "It always creeped me out as a kid."

Jo took him from the bottom rooms, in and out, showing everything, she had done to add to the place, and then took him upstairs. The dogs wanted to come too. She turned to look at them.

"Nos-Ferrah-Tu, stay here cause we are coming right back down. Go get some water, you all need to drink a little more," and she pointed at the bowls, and they all did as they were told.

"Wow, you have them wrapped around your finger," he said, congratulating her.

"Nah, they are just super smart," she said.

They walked upstairs from the back staircase, up to the top, she opened the servant closet proud to show him all the towels, soaps, shower caps and little bottles of shampoos and conditioner.

"Later we will have to brand these little babies, but for now I found a place to buy these in bulk. They are also helping me right now with a logo. As soon as that is done then all these little items will have the logos on them. They'll send me stickers for these ones too," she said looking them over. "Isn't that cool?"

His eyebrows went up, "Very. This is exciting Jo. You really seem happy. I like seeing this on you."

She smiled at him, nodding yes. She liked it too. She walked him down the hall and went into the first bedroom on the right and gave him the tour. They came out of that bedroom and into what was her bedroom.

"Are you going to be renting this out too, your room? You mentioned at dinner you might stay in your room after all" he asked.

"Yes. I am feeling really comfortable in the cottage house, and I made it very homey, so for now at least, that is how I will do it," she said.

He nodded being that it made great sense and she continued the tour.

"Everything looks really good."

They stepped out of the room and Jo began to lead him back down the stairs toward the back staircase. Donovan had stopped, looking at the Cold Room door.

"We aren't going into this room?" he asked.

"Oh, no, not tonight. We are leaving that room alone."

Donovan understood and carried out her orders by catching up and following behind her. The dogs were not the only ones who understood when to be obedient.

As they reached the bottom of the stairs they were greeted by the dogs patiently waiting with smiles.

"Well, hello again little ones," Donovan said to them giving them each a little scratch on the head.

Jo appreciated anyone who gave love to animals.

"So how about those sandwiches?" Donovan asked with a smile. "How about we make them together," he said smiling at her. "Got any chips?"

She smiled ear to ear. *This guy gets it,* she thought to herself jokingly. If he had said Lay's Sour Cream Chips, she'd have thought, *Soul Mates!*

Chapter Twenty-One
Black-Out Tour

"I've scheduled the first tour one week before opening night. Can I post a flyer here at the Cafe?"

"Are you serious," Ginni said incredulously, "of course you can. Give me a bunch and I will get everyone in town that I know to put them up too. Oh my god, this is gonna be so f***ing amazing," she said under her breath not wanting to swear at work. Well, not wanting to be heard swearing at work.

Ginni was so excited about this venture it was endearing. No doubt, her sister was really rubbing off on her. Layce had a shine that was contagious, and Jo could see it on Ginni. It made her heart smile.

"Also, Mamma said they will bake anything you want daily, you just need to let them know and I will deliver it. She said I could even cook the eggs here if I want. That bit is up to you."

"That actually could be good at first and see how it goes," Jo said.

"When will you have the flyers?" Ginni asked.

"Today or tomorrow." Jo was excited, Everything was coming along swimmingly.

"And the yurt? How's it going?"

"It's going. Seems pretty straight forward. They have been at it while I have been at it inside. Team work! They expect it to be done by the weekend."

Ginni smiled, handing Jo her coffee.

"Thank you," Jo said turning to leave, walking toward the exit.

"What date did you set for the formal opening?" Ginni yelled out over a puff of cappuccino steam.

Jo looked back at her standing beneath the door, "March 13th," and she smiled.

Ginni looked up, knowing the tour was set for one week prior. "Wait, so, the tour is on 3/6," she asked and started laughing.

"Why are you laughing?" Jo said with a smile and did not understand why Ginni thought that was funny.

"3/6, three 6's, HELLO, 666!" Ginni yelled out. Others in line and in their seats were alarmed hearing that number. It still had such powerful superstition.

"Jo smiled, "Oh, wow, I didn't even realize that. Awesome!" and she smiled at Ginni with eyebrows raised, shaking her head yes for approval.

"Fuck Yah!" She yelled out. "Oops," she said covering her mouth and looking around apologetically. Employees looked at her and everyone seemed either scared or intrigued. Jo really didn't care which. It was happening. She smiled to herself devilishly and took a sip of her coffee as she walked out.

Chapter Twenty-Two
The Presentation

Johannah had called all the women together to inspect the home, see the yurt, and to discuss the game plan. It was night, the best time for them all to meet after their work day was done.

"Ok, two weeks to opening. One week to tour. Let's go down the list," Jo said.

"This is so exciting," Layce said, slightly jumping up and down and clapping her hands silently.

They all looked at each other, standing in the kitchen in a circle, standing facing each other with excitement.

"Ok, first, let me take you out to the yurt. " Jo wasted no time, she got down to business, secretly eager to share the beauty of everything. Somehow everything had led to this house and these moments, and she felt happy. The darkness of how it all occurred was always there in the shadows, but in moments like these, she could push them to the side. She was allowed to feel joy! Darkness had become her bedfellow.

She led them to the back door from the kitchen, passing the mahogany wood wainscoting, the velvet wallpaper, the hardwood floor, the luxurious rugs, drapes

125

and antique pieces from the house's inception. The ambiance of an ancient home. They all stood at the back door waiting for Jo.

"Ready to see?" she said, They all remained silent and excited, including the dogs who were always underfoot. They made not a sound, simply waited with excited smiles in anticipation.

She opened the back door to blackness save for the glowing light of the moon far off in the distance bouncing off the harbor. She flipped a switch from inside on the wall and a million fairy lights lit up a cobble stone path leading all the way to the yurt. Wild flowers lined the cobble stone path and the lights flickered like fireflies dancing in the moonlight! An audible gasp came from the girls!

The cottage lay off to the left from their view, also having had a cobble stone path made leading to it, and all new landscaping up against its walls and leading down its path. A sign approaching the porch read, Caretaker.

Jo simply led them down the path to the new spa that called to them. They all were silent as they were seduced to move towards it like a moth to flame. It was beautiful.

Approaching the yurt, which was elegantly done, a little porch had been built around it with reclaimed wood,

126

and spindles made into a fence built around it, creating a separate and special feeling. The long cobble path led to the porch. There were two steps leading up into the yurt.

The sign outside the door read:

> *Purdy House Spa,*
> sub header,
> *A Spa Massage, Just For Yurt!*

Beneath that was the name, Layce Begay, Spa Manager and the professional phone line, which was just the home landline number for guests to call. Business would be done from inside the main house and of course, never from inside the yurt, for peace's sake!

Layce got teary eyed. Ginni looked at her quietly and hugged her at the hip while still looking at it. Jo unlocked the door and flipped the switch. More magic.

The ceiling inside of the yurt was draped with flowing white tapestries in a circular pattern from the center flowing out to the yurt's circular frame, showing no sign of the yurt's foundation, fairy lights illuminated from beneath the drapes, electric taper candles perfectly placed in five foot antique cast iron candelabras and table candelabras, the smell of lavender traversed the space from scented sprays on the sheets of the table and dried lavender placed all around the walls in decorative vases

127

mixed with others such as palms and ferns. In the center was a single massage table with luxurious soft sheets, pillows and head rest. A table nearby filled with scented oils and body butter lotions for those who preferred lotion rather than oil. Several amber spray bottles already filled with lavender oil and others oil scents mixed with water to shake and spray in the room before each client.

They walked in and looked around. There had been a half bath installed for a restroom visit and also a place for Layce and the other masseur to wash their hands before and after the service. It was perfectly luxurious and still simple, decorated to match the outer room. Three cast iron candelabras adorned the walls of the bathroom, each holding six taper candles that flickered on the wall (electric of course) all controlled by a single remote. In such a small space, there would never be a need to even turn on the light, except from cleaning. The light of the candles created a golden glow.

A brochure tray was outside the door of the yurt, stuck to the wall in a plexiglass tray, and another on the booking table in the entrance for those wishing to peek in during off hours and pick up a brochure, as well as for Layce to book and rebook clients. The service would be open to the community, not just guests, so she envisioned a busy and thriving spa.

Layce picked up the brochure from the outside tray and moved over to the bench right outside the door and sat down to take a look. Jo joined her on the bench and Ginni leaned back on the railing. It was a beautiful night. Layce touched the spa brochure feeling the glossy paper, and she brushed her hand across it in awe.

"I didn't realize until now, sissy, that you gave me a career." She looked at her sister gratefully.

Jo looked at her inquisitively.

"Before, I have always felt like one of a million massage therapists and like I had this license, but still felt like I have been aimless for some reason. Business has never been great anywhere I have gone, so it has always been, just getting by. But I see this and realize you gave my career a direction in a snap of your fingers. How did you do that?" she said, smiling and moving over to hug her.

Jo hugged her back. "Well, you deserve it and I need you. So, it's mutually beneficial. You aren't one of a million, you are one in a million! You are to me... to us," she said and looked at Ginni who agreed.

Layce looked back at the menu. Then closer at the logo.

"Ooh," Ginni said leaning in to look closer..

Layce studied it.

129

"The house, it's blurry in the picture sis," she said, not taking her eye off of it.

Jo smiled a facetious smile. "I know, just enough to see, but not clearly, and just enough to feel off kilter. It makes you feel slightly uneasy, right?"

"Ooh, yah! Now I get it. I LOVE it!" She exclaimed smiling.

"It felt wrong when I did it," Jo said, "so I knew it was right!" and they all laughed! At that Layce and Jo stood and began walking to go inside the yurt and Ginni followed.

They all broke up and took a minute to investigate every inch of the yurt. They all were mesmerized, like a spell had been cast over them. They opened and closed everything, looked at every product, curtain and oil. Touched every fabric feeling the softness of the fabrics under their fingers, looked at every piece of wood following it to the next area, smelled every scent of lavender, citrus, even chocolate that smelled like tootsie rolls. Admiringly, they studied the flames in the candelabras, the cast iron that held them. Each on their own time looked up as though gazing at the stars, getting lost in the symbiosis of the layers of tapestry woven with the lights that flickered gently beneath them on the ceiling, cascading and moving creating a dream like state of magic.

130

Finally, they all made their way back to one another in the center around the massage table. The luxurious and almost gothic décor made the centerpiece, the table, the offering of the room. A soul offered for such beauty in the guise of a massage. The room seemed to feed in its own way.

"We should continue the tour in the house," Jo said.

"Yah, we should. What time is it, anyway?" Lacye asked.

They left the yurt, the Victorian gothic spa, and once outside, Ginni looked at her phone for the time. Ginni froze. Mouth gaping.

"What?" Ginni said to herself, but out loud.

"What?" Layce asked looking at her. Jo's eyes also switched from the door as she locked it, to Ginni.

"It's after 11 pm. We got here a little after 8, like, a few minutes ago."

They all froze, letting the words sink in a few seconds, then looking back into the spa.

"Oh, no," Jo said in a foreboding voice.

"What's happening? I don't understand." Layce said, confused, looking at them both.

"We lost time, Layce! The yurt is a fricken portal too."

"Oh, great," Layce said throwing up her hands and then slamming her arms down by her sides. "How am I supposed to stay on track with sixty-minute massages in a fricken portal?"

They all burst out laughing, even though it wasn't funny. Could it be that the strangeness had become so normal that they were being sucked into an abnormal way of thinking? Oh, God!

After they all stopped laughing, they walked back toward the house. It seemed so obvious now, they all were lost in their thoughts, and now they knew, for hours, not minutes, they traveled the room touching everything, feeling everything, smelling everything.

"I will have a guy install an annunciator panel with a timer. You will set it for sixty minutes and the light will gently flash at sixty minutes, just in case, with a slight chime. When you start we will test this out, and I will also keep track of time for you to make sure it is fail safe.

Layce nodded her head in agreement. "But is that gonna work Jo?"

"I sure hope so. I'm afraid I'm out of my lane with time warps Layce. This is so weird! We'll figure it out," Jo said reassuringly, only now realizing that the dogs never went into the yurt with them. As they walked back on the pebble stone path she looked to see that they sat in the

132

garden midway between the house and the yurt, off the walkway, facing them in the yurt, silent, huddled but not agitated, just, not going in or too close to the yurt. She hadn't noticed being so distracted with her presentation. The dogs already knew. She made a mental note, *must pay better attention to dogs before entering somewhere.*

She then wondered if she had gotten charged extra for the portal installation from Ginni's uncle's friend, Guy? Lol. It really wasn't funny! She really should be more serious, this was not expected or wanted. Was she trying to create another safe zone and it was just one too many for the ever-present shadow of death in the main house?

Perhaps! But Jo was a problem solver and always had a workaround!

"Boo back, bitch!" She thought to herself before leading them back into the main house.

___

133

Chapter Twenty-Three
Pre-Tour Opening: 666

She woke up like any other day and instead of making her coffee in the cottage, she went into the house. Stepping outside her beautiful cottage and looking left at the yurt, she smiled and felt a moment of this thing happening to her life, magic. A feeling like she was living in an alternate universe than she ever was before. The feeling that she could exist solely on the haunted grounds of her home, yet she knew that was the allure of the place and its curse. It had a seductive power to isolate you. In life, it was called depression. In her house, it was called evil. It was Ada. Even alphabetically her name was a six. A, first in the alphabet, one, and D, fourth. ADA-1+4+1=6. And today, the pre-tour opening of her haunted house of tragedy, March 6th, 3/6=three sixes, 666. This had darkness written all over it. Coincidence? She doubted it. Was the girl guiding this process or did she hate it.

Jo made sure to make this experience a safeguard for her to not be pulled into the current of darkness and begin isolating herself from the world. She had made it possible to bring the world to her and in so doing, would never be left to Ada alone to feed off, to deceive or pull into her insanity and darkness.

134

She walked down her newly pretty walkway of flowers that led to the back door of her house and up the steep stairs. She fobbed her way into the house without a hitch and went to make coffee in the kitchen.

"Well, today's the day," she said out loud, almost as though she knew the little devil was listening, as she scooped coffee into the maker. Why did she continually poke the bear? Perhaps it was her bravery and pure stubbornness to let anyone drive her life in a direction she wasn't willing to go. She couldn't control tragedy, but she could control what happened after.

The rotary phone rang.

"Mom," Jo said, with excitement in her voice. "So good to hear from you." The line was staticky for a moment.

"I'm flying home today from Santa Fe with Mr. Ken," Lorna said, drawing out his name and flaunting her girl power at her age. Lorna had mentioned seeing a fella when she had visited Jo on her first visit to the house not long ago and mentioned enjoying her golden years. She had been single so long raising Layce and Jo and had never remarried or had any sort of soulful relationship with anyone after their father had died when the girls were young.

"Mr. Ken Huh? Get it Mom," Jo teased. They both had a chuckle. "Is this the same one that you said was dapper and looked like Cary Grant with thick framed black glasses and grey hair?"

"Oh, ya, that's him alright," she said sassily. This put a smile on Jo's face.

"Did you enjoy your time there? I love Santa Fe."

"Oh yes, it was the best, as usual," Lorna said appraisingly. "Mr. Ken had never been here, so he loved it. You know, I was thinking of moving out here. He said he thought it would be nice to live here too."

"Mom are you already talking about moving in together?" Jo said with only a tinge of concern.

"Well, if he wants to come along and be my boy toy he's welcome to. But you know, everything is gonna be in my name. That's just how I roll," Lorna said.

There was that fire Jo inherited from her mother that she so enjoyed. Just when she thought she might get concerned for her mother, Lorna flashed her strength, rational fortitude that swayed the rising concern. She knew what she was doing. Plus, Jo believed she should have fun after all life had put her through. She deserved to have two loving daughters and a boyfriend after losing a husband and spending all that time raising children alone. She paid for all her sins upfront if she had any and had credits of pleasure

136

to last a lifetime. She deserved it and should live it up in her golden years, Jo thought.

"Well, we can talk more about that later. I wanted to call to say good luck! Of course, your sister told me every detail of every second I have missed over there. You know your sister, she does love to share all the moments," Lorna said endearingly, and they both laughed at the understatement. "Well, good, cause I don't think I would have had the energy to. It's been a lot."

"Are you ready?" Lorna asked.

Just as she did, the doorbell rang, right before Ginni and Layce opened and came in.

"Yah, I think so. It's a new endeavor so it will be on-the-job training but it's all mine. So, I can make changes as we go."

"That's my girl," Lorna said with love in her voice. "You know, you have always been one to forge your own path. You're a leader Jo, and all this ... is some strange universal web, it's all meant to be ..." and her voice dropped off.

Jo shook her head in silence. She knew her Mom was on the other end doing the very same thing.

"Well, reinforcements are here," Jo said.

"Oh, good, let me talk to Layce," she asked.

"Ok, hold on," Jo said.

"Layce," she said holding up the phone with the curling cord hanging down, "It's Mom."

Layce's eyes got big, and she jumped up and ran over to the phone, taking it from Jo's hand. Jo laughed at her unending enthusiasm for even the smallest of things.

"MOMMY," she said into the phone smiling, and they began a quick chat.

Soon the conversation was over, and they all were alone together.

"We need to walk the route, say the words loosely, and generally rehearse the flow to get the choreography right," Jo said, looking at Layce.

Layce nodded her head and added, "Yah, we were talking also," she motioned to Ginni, "that Ginni should learn and go over all this too, so we have a back up in case someone ever gets sick or goes on vacation or takes a day off. Ginni agreed to be a back up for now," Layce explained.

"That's amazing, Ginni. Thank you!" she said giving a caring smile to Ginni. "Ok, it starts in the line to keep things moving. I have put a small table at the front gate. I will be handing out liability waivers to everyone in line. As people enter they will hand in signed waivers. If they don't sign it, they don't get in," Jo said.

"Ok, what if someone gets to the front entrance and they are still reading their form, holding up the line?" Layce asked.

"Whoever ends up doing this part from now to whenever these will be the rules. Anyone who doesn't sign or is still reading is told to go to the back of the line until they're ready. Don't rush them to sign. I don't want to hear anyone later making an argument that we forced them to sign. We will force them to the back of the line, and you can't get sued for that." They all nodded their heads in agreement.

"Besides," Jo said, "the waiver is gonna be short and sweet, so we shouldn't really ever run into that issue, but you know how I am, 'Over plan, rather than underdeliver'."

"Right," Layce said professionally.

Jo continued. "From the gate, I will make sure everyone had placed their waiver in the tray. Groups of five to seven will be allowed in together. I want the groups to be manageable. Ideally five but will increase up to seven for groups that came together. Sound good?" she asked Layce who would be the one doing the first tour.

"Yes, that sounds good," Layce said seriously, shaking her head.

"The tour from start to finish is about fifteen minutes. I have set up the website for the real thing to allow time slots to be booked so they sell out and we have control over the crowds. I'll schedule three tours per hour leaving fifteen minutes free for catching your breath and bathroom break the last part of the hour. So back-to-back the first three and break. So, there will be a total of nine-night tours from five pm to eight pm. When you get to the bottom of the stairs and the tour is over I will have the next group outside the front door waiting for you to get, and I will take the group you just toured out. We'll see how that flows." Layce nodded.

"By the way," Ginni asked. "How are your neighbors with this? Speaking of crowds."

"Well," Jo said," I have seen some during the process of building, putting up signs and taking out the trash and the ones I have spoken to seem just as eager to get inside and see. I assured them that it will be very controlled so there isn't a bunch of unruly people outside lingering. Keeping it that way will be judged on how well I make that happen so it's always gonna be in my mind. We don't need things to get out of control or neighbors will get upset."

The girls both nodded their heads in agreement.

"I will open up appointments for the spa hours and the tours tonight just before we give the first tour. I would imagine they will begin to talk and then people will go over to the website to book limited tours. And by the way, no money will ever be exchanged on site. It's all done online. If anyone doesn't like it, too bad!" Jo said.

"Exactly," Ginni said.

"Ok, perfect. I have stanchions leading out the back door and back into the front away from the main line. The route we mapped out, Layce, is perfect in and out. Stay on track, no extra talking unless you're moving through the tour. If people ask you a question that requires a long answer, just say, 'That's a great question', you can be cheeky and say, 'If I tell you, I'll have to kill you', then raise your eyebrows playfully aware of your cliché, then while moving answer as best you can," Jo said. "If there is something you don't know, it's okay to say you don't know, sis, but acknowledge it's a great question to find out and thank them for it. Maybe you can say something like the house still has many secrets we are uncovering. Something like that. It's okay to not know everything about the house. It will take time to know the details of this house. I suspect their questions will give us more to think about."

"I will keep track of questions like that as well so perhaps later we can put a book or something together that we can sell, or even a brochure of Q&A," Layce said.

"That sounds good," Jo said. "Ooh, or even an extended tour.

They walked from the front of the house, down the hallway, up the back stairs, down the hall and through each room, leading to the Cold Room, the entrance into the main room, then into the Cold Room itself. Back down the hall and down the front stairs where all the teeth poured like rain, passing through the dining room and kitchen, pointing to the teeth in the jar, then exiting the back route and following the stanchions out.

"Oh, I also almost forgot to tell you, but Guy made me two custom ramps that push up on both stairs on the side for handicap accessibility. Although there is nothing that can be done to go upstairs once in, we can grant access into the house itself. This is also for the stay portion of the B&B, downstairs rooms."

"Excellent," Ginni and Layce both said in unison and then smiled and laughed at one another.

They walked and talked the path several times. They were ready.

"I'm nervous," Layce explained.

"Me too," Jo said. "Isn't it wonderful?"

They all smiled deviously.

Chapter Twenty-Four
5 PM! The Tours Begin

The Pre-tour was set to go live a few days before the opening and Ginni no doubt had been putting it on blast to every customer that came through Mamma's Café. Layce was telling everyone she knew from the spa as she ended her employment. The town had been abuzz with the news that they would be able to see this truly haunted house where a community tragedy had occurred. Whether they experienced a paranormal event or not was beside the point. They were going to get to go inside the most beautiful house where multiple tragedies occurred, and a child serial killer lived and did her demented work. That in itself was worth the twenty-five-dollar ticket.

Not only that, but Geraldine stopped by just before opening delivering the plaque and affixing it to the iron pole at the gate just before the tours began. Just like kismet, something divine in nature was happening here; everything was fitting together like some determined yet divine nightmare puzzle playing out to their delight. Was it wrong to feel happy and excited showing off such a home, such a tragedy? As far as Jo was concerned, no. She had no choice but to make lemonade and she did just that.

143

An hour before showtime, everyone and thing was in place.

"Geraldine, you are amazing. Thank you so much for putting that plaque up. Perfect timing. Its official," she said looking out at the pole with a smile and then at Geraldine. "Thank you. I will look at it officially when I go out to greet the group. Wow, so amazing!"

"May I help or do anything dear? I want to help in some way if I can," Geraldine asked.

"Oh, um, sure," Jo replied. "You can wait in the back Cold Room for the people to come in and wave hello," she laughed at Geraldines body language.

Geraldine's eyes got big, "Anything else, dear?" and they both giggled.

"Sure. All joking aside, you can remain in the kitchen and help me take the tour guests outside when the tour is over and point them in the right direction. The stanchions will guide them out of the house and across the driveway beyond the gates, but you can make sure no one goes off course and into the garden and yurt area," Jo said.

"Oh, wonderful. I'll get my mom voice ready," Geraldine said and smiled. "Can I make you some tea or coffee.

"How about some coffee. I need to go meet with Layce for our pre-game huddle."

144

"Ok, I'll make some coffee and just be here ready when you are," Geraldine said.

"Perfect," Jo said and walked toward Layce who was going through her flash cards and looking nervous standing in the library by the front door. She was in an all-black lace, high neck dress, looking the part.

"You look amazing Layce. Wow, you look the part, very … Victorian. How do you feel?"

"Oh, like I'm gonna have diarrhea any moment and forget everything," she said, nervously laughing.

Jo burst out in a quick laugh before recovering. "Layce, remember, this is the test run so it's all good. If you forget anything just tell them some of our own stories and that will get you through. You know the history. Talk about how it feels in here and feel free to make it personal. We are real people. Also pay attention to how you feel because there is that element of not knowing when *atmosphere* will arrive and then it's all rules off. Remember that they have no idea what you are supposed to say. So, if you forget this or that, they have no idea. You don't have to do or achieve anything. Simply walk them through a beautiful home with horrible memories!"

"Yes, okay, I feel better," Layce said relieved and exhaling. "Very skull and bones pep-talk, perfect! It worked!" And she meant it.

"Put the cards away, now, sis. You are a cheerleader for this house. Just be you, okay? You got this? Now I'm gonna go check on the dogs in the cottage and change into a black dress like you," and she walked away toward the back door of the house. "By the way," she yelled out. Geraldine who was making coffee also looked over to Jo. "Every slot on the tour is booked! " She and Geraldine smiled, Geraldine gave a thumbs up and a big teeth smile.

"Oh God." Layce whispered nervously under her breath, fooling with her collar in the mirror. "I got this," she said in the mirror in the library, and she put the flash cards in the top drawer or the demilune now that she was just gonna riff it! Well, sort of. "I know this house," she said gazing into the mirror. I know its story. I'm part of its story. I know this house!"

Johannah came out of her cottage, having fed Nos-Ferah-Tu and changed into a slinky dress that was goth and dark. She even found a black cameo her mother had given her and placed it at her collar. She looked stunning. Ruby red lipstick like blood. Vintage 1960s witchy pointed toe red patten leather shoes with three cascading horizontal infinity symbols on the toes, smallest to largest leading to a slight part in the leather showing just the right amount of toe cleavage, an adjustable strap and two-inch heels. She was sexy, but also not a masochist. Black fish net stockings with a seam down the back of her legs. It was perfect.

When she entered the back doorway into the house, to her surprise she had another visitor standing in the kitchen.

Layce yelled out excitedly, "DeeDee is here."

Jo looked over to see Dr. Donovan or DeeDee, standing with Geraldine, with a coffee in his hand. Geraldine offered her a cup, but she politely shooed it away, there was no time now.

"So, if anyone has a psychotic break (me) then we have mental health support!" Layce said, then going back to her pacing and recitation. They all giggled!

Jo looked over at Donovan and smiled warmly at him. It felt nice to have such support. Just as she said that she heard the back door screen slam and Ginni walked in.

"Hey, bitches! Oh, look," she said, looking around. "We're all here!"

It made Jo's heart swell seeing her family all in the room together. It was go time and everyone she cared about was there.

"Amazing!" she said out loud. "Thank you for all being here," and she took a deep breath.

"Jo, come look at this," Layce said, and they all walked over to the door to peek out. The cast iron fence was lined with people holding their papers and excitedly chattering to get the tour.

"Wow, this could really work out," Donovan said smiling!

Jo just laughed. "Ok, Ginni and I will go outside and get people ready. Note to self, tell people from this point on to stay in their cars until fifteen minutes before the tour. I don't want the neighbors to get mad at me."

Donovan nodded.

"We are booked for nine tours, seven each group, sixty-three total guests, three tours per hour at fifteen minutes, and it looks like they're all outside now. Eek!" Jo said.

"There's a news van interviewing people," Layce yelled out.

"Oh, God, this is really happening," Jo said. "Ok, places everyone. Fifteen minutes to opening. Geraldine and Donovan keep your places please in the kitchen, Ginni, you're with me, Layce, you got this, sister," and she hugged a bear hug around her sister.

When Johannah opened the door and stepped out on the porch the crowd erupted in applause.

"Oh, my goodness," was all Ginni could say.

Jo took it in like a peach! "Smile and wave, Ginni" Jo instructed. "I will work the front of the line and bring the first group up. You make sure the next group is ready with their forms and say hello to the people in line. Get a feel for them and then you can tell me later anything you heard. Also, feel free to do an interview if you like. Would you mind?" Jo asked her.

"Heck, yah, I will do an interview," she replied.

"Thank you for everything, Ginni, truly. Opening night, I need to be focused on the flow and prefer to do a more formal interview with them in the house. Layce is really nervous. Poor thing, all the pressure is on her. You can let them know to schedule it with me directly. I could even do a private limited tour on camera. Tell them to call me tomorrow! I mean, if they ask."

"You got it, boss," Ginni said playfully, and they both walked down the stairs with Jo, the madame of the house getting all the attention as if a vampire had just walked out into the light. Ginni followed behind like her faithful familiar, also all dressed in black and with a skull and bones necktie.

149

Chapter Twenty-Five
There They Stood

Johannah was elegant and seemingly made for this role. Ginni worked the crowd and said hello to literally everyone, she knew just about everyone in line. The first group was stanchioned off with a red velvet rope at the front of the line and all had given Jo their liability forms. She was not responsible for anything that could or would occur on her property, she was not responsible for lost or stolen items, she was not responsible for heart attacks or sudden death, nightmares, trips, falls, injuries, the liability form was iron clad from the local attorney which also included no refunds for any reason. Another one of Ginni's amazing referrals. They also could not take video; however, photos were allowed.

Forms collected, she placed the liability forms in the lock box under the small table attached to the iron gate she had installed and turned the lock to the box, and then closed it in behind a door, which she locked with the skeleton key she had on her bracelet.

"Ready all?" she asked the tour group behind the red velvet stanchion. She could see many, even some of her neighbors' adult children in the first group. A group of seven, some who came together and some who came in a

150

couple. They all nodded quietly as though a cat had gotten their tongue. Neighbors stood outside on their grass waving to her when they could catch her eyes. She simply smiled, not wanting to break character.

"How many of you are nervous … even scared?" she asked them. Some hands went up, some nods, some seemed so scared they could only make eye contact with eyes like black buttons.

"Well, I can promise you a history of tragedy and show you where it all took place, but I cannot promise you a paranormal witness, nor can I say you won't be touched or even lifted, God forbid … thrown from where you stand, as I was, in the hall leading to the Cold Room. What I definitely can promise you is a fascinating few minutes … Ready?" They all nodded yes, terrified, and she opened her end of the stanchion and asked them to follow her to the front porch.

Like kids in a candy shop, they soaked up every part of the house visually, its off energy, some felt the chill of the windows like eyes from the Cold Room looking down upon them, some looked at the ghostly grounds and knowing they were going into not only a place of beauty, but one where a vile tragedy did occur. They were going to see a piece of history from their own town, one which

151

they would know a little more intimately after their visit to the Purdy House Stay and Tours.

She led them to the front porch, and they soaked up every bit of the house and its surrounding like kids gobbling sugar. She felt their rush of energy, and they weren't even in the house yet. For a brief moment with her back to them she worried what that energy would do mixed in such an unpredictable house. But it was too late now. It was happening, and she wasn't liable.

Music! She had forgotten to put on atmospheric sound themed for dark and eerie. Every setting was better with music. But as she took the step to the front porch, she heard a faint music low enough to be heard but not so low there was silence. Layce had taken care of it!

She turned to face them, to see all seven standing on the front porch. She looked out to see all those in line excitedly watching her and the group in a hushed silence of anticipation mixed with nervous giggles. Beyond their faces she could see in the distance her neighbors, riveted and excited just as she was.

"And now, my friends, let's begin. I am one of only four caretakers of this house and I will not be the last. When my bones are dead and buried, another will take my place as this home's caretaker, and so on, and so on, and so on…she faded out

"And now I shall deliver you into the hands of Queen Layce, the Manager of Guest Tours. She is as unpredictable as the house ... Good luck," she said and held the door open for the guests to enter. They ushered into their doom. She closed the front porch and turned away to hear Layce say,

"Oh, dearly departed souls. You have no idea what you have just gotten yourself in to. But no matter, it's too late now!" She said devilishly. "How many of you are scared shitless!" Eyes bulged, but she was not going to be woke or corporate. "A show of hands, please," she said as though she were a southern belle.

Every hand went up and she laughed at them.

"Good, then let's get a move on. We'll pass many rooms and doors, but we all know you are here for one room and one door in particular, so let's not dittle dattle, shall we?" and she turned to move them down the hall, pointing out rooms, books, wallpaper, some history of the home belonging to the original settlers of Gig Harbor, details of the home in a nonchalant way that seemed as though she had done this her whole life. Layce was made for this. Just as Jo was meant to be the caretaker of this home, this beautifully dark home.

"Touch nothing," she said sternly to one guest about to reach out and touch the velvet wallpaper. Then

153

delicately, "You don't want to take something home with you, do you?" she said in a playfully serious tone and circled the bend of the banister, and up they went on the back staircase, moving closer to the Cold Room..

Jo looked back to see Geraldine and Donovan who kept themselves out of sight, but then they peeked out at Jo once Layce was out of sight and nodded their heads, as impressed with Layce as she was.

"Queen Layce," Donovan said, "That was a good one." He smiled his Keanu Reeves smile that melted her heart for a moment. *Snap out of it!*

"Yes, agreed," Geraldine said, "I rather think it adds to her mystique don't you?" she asked Donovan and they both agreed, sipping some coffee.

Jo smiled at them. They were all a bunch of kids playing grownup.
"You both know what to do when they come down the front staircase?" she asked them, making sure they were prepared. She didn't wait for an answer. "Layce will lead them to the living room and then out the back door following the stanchions."

"Oh, yes, dear. DeeDee and I have got it." She said smiling at him. Somewhere along the line they had become partners in crime.

154

"Can I call you that, Donovan?" she asked, so close to his face from hiding behind the wall.

Donovan simply smiled and nodded. She smiled back and they both waved at her. She turned and stepped back out on the porch and the crowd became excited again. The sun was setting and so much of it was already behind the lush landscape of trees in the neighborhood. The orange glow of lights that had been put outside the home sporadically mixed with the fairy lights created a magical look that would come alive at night. Everything was on a timer. Mood and music was heavily considered in this venture.

She walked to the iron gate taking her time and feeling the eyes of the terrible girl above on her back. She stood in front of the empty corral, having just led the last seven to their doom, and asked the next group of seven to step up and into the victims' corral as Ginni opened her end of the stanchion and let the next seven in. They were now trapped in velvet rope.

"How many of you have any idea what you are about to walk into?" she asked. Nervous eyes glanced at each other without speaking a word.

"Good, the silent suffering types," she nodded playfully. "Hand in your death certificates, ahem, I mean, your liability forms," she said, facetiously correcting herself.

155

She was having too much fun with this, and it was all happening so effortlessly. Kismet?

Just then a scream and a slamming door came from the Cold Room above and the crowd gasped. Jo was startled and the guests also saw it, making them even more nervous.

Ginni looked horrified. The corral of the next victims looked at Jo scared and waiting for her to say something. All she could muster was shaking her head and calm as a butterfly.

"Foolish mortals," she said shaking her head and looking down at her fabulous red witchy shoes. "Foolish, foolish mortals. I had no idea what I was getting into, but you," she said light heartedly, "you are paying to walk into it." She smiled a smile with no teeth.

One woman in a couple was experiencing second thoughts and wanted out of the corral as her boyfriend tried to convince her to stay, Ginni lifted the velvet rope to let her pass.

"Dear, dear," Jo said quietly shaking her head. "No refunds," she spoke out loud in a devilish tone that sounded like Elvira! "Anyone else wish to pass away through the velvet rope?"

Just then she caught a glimpse of her neighbors across the street, now sitting in zero gravity chairs with a drink with an umbrella in it, laugh and holding their mouth to calm lower the sound of their chuckle. Jo just smiled and played coy. The neighbors were being entertained and she loved it.

A few minutes passed and the couple returned.

Ginni went to let them back into the velvet corral. "Are you sure, friend? This tour isn't for sissies," she told the woman.

Jo wanted to laugh but she simply looked down.

"Yes, I'm sure. I can do this,." The tour guest answered. Ginni smiled and let them back in."

"Yes, dear, a woman can do all sorts of things: hammer their father's head in like Lizzy Bordan, or even grow to be an over achieving serial killer. It's limitless, really!" she said, shaking her head really playing the part of devilishly humorous.

The group laughed and the mood settled. The groups behind were even more excited to go in and although Jo was curious about the scream and slamming door, she wasn't surprised, it had become her new normal to have weird things happen in the home. She was excited to ask what happened at the end of the night and get the reaction of the tour guests.

The liability forms were locked away for group two and the red velvet stanchion freed her next batch of

157

victims, walking cautiously behind her like the last group, having no idea what they were getting themselves into.

Layce appeared at the door; the introduction, pass off skit repeated. Layce was slightly flushed but more focused. Whatever happened, she was ready for it and seemed to be even stronger for it. Jo relaxed. She made the pass and it repeated again.

Geraldine was back in place and Donovan was gone, and she knew that meant he was taking care of the outside group exiting.

Just then she heard the group voice swell with an "aw" of surprise and a thump! Fear flashed on Geraldine's face for just a moment. Then they heard nervous laughter. The bizarre music added to the spooky ambiance of the elegant Victorian home.

"What the hell?" Jo whispered to Geraldine across the way.

"I have no idea, dear. So weird. I'm just glad it isn't me."

"Yes, well, you had a dress rehearsal, didn't you?" Jo smiled. "Ok, heading back out to my next victims," Jo said to her and smiled.

"Okay, dear," Geraldine said and then looked out the kitchen window catching a glimpse of something.

Jo's eyebrows creased curiously looking at Geraldine.

"Oh, boy, there are several news stations talking to Ginni right now. Cameras and lights and everything." She turned back around letting go of the curtain and looking at Jo. "It's strange, isn't it, Jo? To have all this tragedy turn into a fun circus for others?" She was contemplating quietly. There was no judgement in her statement, merely a thought of how strange the world was.

"And a business?" Jo added. "Yah ... it's fucking weird," she said, and quickly pinched her lips shut for cussing while talking to a senior. That was rude in her upbringing. "Sorry, Geraldine," she said, "for being disrespectful." Jo had great manners that she sometimes forgot.

"No, I totally agree" Geraldine said in her feminine quiet way. "Fucking weird," she said drawing out the words mimicking Jo. "But ... fun!" she said enthusiastically.

With that Jo went out to resume her role as caretaker of the home that called out to her from its tragedy, while she had been in the midst of her own! A strange pair indeed. Two worlds, past and present colliding their horrors.

Chapter Twenty-Six
Slamming Doors, Neighbors and Huddles

The night before had been amazingly wonderful, albeit exhausting, and Jo had already planned to have Layce and Ginni over for a late breakfast to go over the details and finetune the machine, something she imagined she would do as often as needed to make it all work for them and their guests.

She was buzzing with excitement and had hardly slept with the happiness she felt for the future. She had a whole new focus, and it was wonderful, despite the fact that her new focus had kind of hijacked her life that was already a mess. But Jo was a lemonade maker. Anywhere, anytime someone gave her lemons, boom, lemonade. She didn't settle for what others delivered when she didn't like it. She made decisions to make things work a different way.

She took Nos-Ferrah-Tu out for a walk and went out of the cottage, down the side driveway that still had stanchions up and went out to walk her fur babies around the block before the girls got there.

The neighbors who were watching the night before were out watering their lawns and the street was clean, almost no sign of crowds, and that was a good thing.

Her funny neighbors across the street who had been in zero gravity chairs enjoying the entertainment seemed to be out already, just hoping to run into her. She crossed the street with the dogs to say hello and chat.

The wife waved her over excitedly. Jo smiled at her, and her husband finished watering the plants and turned off the hose and walked over.

"That was the most entertaining thing I've watched in a while. You were hilarious. I hope you don't mind our eavesdropping?" she asked. "We were just so excited for you."

"Aw, thank you. I feel strange not knowing your names. I'm Jo. And you both are?"

"Hank and Moody," she said pointing to one another. Oddly, she was Hank, and he was Moody, and Jo loved that!

"I love your names," she said to Hank and Moody.

"So, you need to know that we are huge monster lovers, anything haunted, etc. So, we are huge fans of what you are doing and intend to stay at your B&B, even though you're across the street. We just think it's such a great idea to open up the history to our town."

Jo smiled brightly while Moody also looked at her and jovially nodded his head in agreement.

Sufani Weisman-Garza

"We go to Monsterpalooza, Son of Monsterpalooza, Midsummer Scream, HORRORCON and such, so we are really into it." Her smile was so warm and approving.

Perfect neighbors, kitty corner to her on the corner house. *Excellent!*

"If you ever need help with anything we're in. Holiday decorating, even a hand working the tours, I have some time on my hands, and I could always help."

"That sounds great. We're gonna have our first meeting today in just a bit, and I am certain I will need more help. I will let you know. Thank you so much for your support. I really appreciate it. Well, off we go," and she shook the three leashes in her hands. The dogs were eager to smell everything under the sun and were having a ball with the neighbors' flowers and fire hydrant dog communication pole. They said their goodbyes and she continued on her blissful walk. The day was beautiful!

There was a knock on the front door. Layce and Ginni looked through the screen.

"Come in," she yelled out, busy in the kitchen making them a continental breakfast.

"We can't," Layce said and jimmied the doorknob that wouldn't budge.

162

Jo put down what she was doing and walked over to the door and opened it easily. Nothing was said, it was becoming normal. They all went back into the kitchen. Jo resumed what she was doing.

"Oh my gosh, I'm so tired. That was so awesome, though," Layce exclaimed.

Jo began serving plates and the toast popped. Ginni wandered over and began buttering and assisting Jo with the plating.

"Hello," a man's voice rang out from the back door. DeeDee just opened the door and came in. Jo's eyebrows lifted as the front doorbell rang.

"Yoohoo," Geraldine was at the front door. Everyone's heads were like watching a tennis match.

"Enter," Layce said playfully, and Geraldine came over. Ginni pulled more plated for the new arrivals.

"Well, hello everyone," Jo said, suddenly the CEO of her dining room table.

"We're here to see how it went," Geraldine said with excitement, sitting down and being served a plate by Ginni. They all had food and coffee now and Jo could see that Donovan and Geraldine conspired to show up in the morning, that was clear. They were officially in cahoots. It was cute!

163

Jo sat back and had coffee and cherished what was in her cup. Steam billowed and she closed her eyes. The rest all did the same like follow the leader and there was a hush at the table.

"Ok, that was the most fun thing I think I have ever done. I felt like Elvira with the guests out front," Jo said. "Layce, how was it for you?"

"Well, I felt so much pressure at the beginning but once I did the first tour I kind of got into it and then some weird stuff did happen that scared the guests, and it made me laugh internally. But before we go into that, can I ask, Jo, that we lessen the tour group from three an hour to two? I found we needed just a little more time in the tour to not feel rushed."

"Done," Jo said. I haven't released the tour and B&B booking yet. I wanted to talk to you first, to get feedback. I will make those changes and then let you know when we go live okay."

"Great," Layce said, smiling and kicking her feet back and forth under the table like a sweet little girl.

"Eat, everyone, please," Jo said with a hand gesture around the table. They dug in.

"Oh," Donovan said finishing up his egg and wiping his mouth with the napkin, "We," he looked at Geraldine, "think that you need a gift shop, so the guests go straight

164

from the house into the gift shop to extend their tour. It will feel longer because they can stay on the grounds longer and they may want a souvenir."

"Oh, yes," Layce said. "Guests did seem to want something after the tour and would have appreciated staying a little longer, I think."

"Agreed," Ginni said.

"Ginni, did you hear anything as people were leaving or people in line talking about anything pertinent?" Jo asked.

"Yah, a few couples asked if there was a gift shop and I overheard people saying they wish they could stay longer on the grounds to look around."

"Ok, let's do it. I will have to hire someone for the tour gift shop."

"ME," Ginni said. Everyone looked at Ginni. She was so abrupt and over the moon for the position.

"Ginni, how can you work all day at Mamma's and then evenings here? That's too much," Jo said with concern for her balance.

"I was thinking that I would just do the catering for you here and I could do that too. Mamma's is not my dream job, but this … this could be, because I'm part of this special creation and family." She looked around the table and at the room they were in. "I could be the Food and Fun Manager!" she said and smiled.

"Are you sure, Ginni?" Jo said surprised.

"Heck, yah," she said and looked at Layce for approval which she quickly gave.

"Ok, then," Jo said. "Ginni, you will be the food and fun manager and handle the B&B meals we've already discussed but you can do it all here so you're on the grounds and can help guests while you are in the kitchen. The nights we have tours you can be in the gift shop. I was thinking the easy fix is to use the inside of the spa area and section off an area to use just for the gifts. No building necessary. We can use stanchions to do that for now. Thoughts?"

Everyone nodded their heads in agreement. Everyone she cared about again was at the table, except for her mom. She'd call her soon to get her back out there to visit.

"We have a week before real opening so I will get the gift shop items for quick and inexpensive souvenirs, t-shirts, hats, key chains to start. The brand company I am working with is very fast. Ginni, if you want, you can help me with the gift shop arrangement and setup and of course you will be paid for last night and moving forward. I also set up an app for clocking in and out so anytime you

166

work, please do that. I will email you the details of payday and all the stuff later today to make it all official. Donovan and Geraldine, you were so helpful last night, supporting me. I always knew you were behind the wall hiding until the guests passed through. Thank you for that. Oh, but, Ginni, you were so helpful with crowd control. What will I do without you?" and then her eyes bulged. "Hank!" she called out.

"Who's Hank?" Donovan asked.

"Ooh, DeeDee," Layce said, not finishing her statement that said, *jealous?*

"Ginni, remember the funny neighbors across the street in zero gravity chairs watching us like entertainment and laughing?"

"Yah," Ginni said.

"Well, this morning I introduced myself. I swear they were out just waiting for me to come by with the dogs. Anyway, nicest couple, Hank, is the wife! Hank and Moody," she announced. "They are so fun, totally into monster culture and were loving it. She would be perfect to help me in the line and even take over for me as madame when I need a break or just have other things to do. She offered to help me this morning. How cool how this is working out?"

"Kismet," Geraldine said. They all fell into silence with smiles, eating and drinking.

"Ginni, give Mamma's proper notice though," she said forking her scrambled egg and taking a bite. "You can be between us while you exit, right?"

Ginni nodded. "Of course."

"Layce and Ginni, I will email all details to you later and, Ginni, after this maybe we can go into the spa to section out the gift shop? Maybe we can call it the 'Spirit Shop'? Layce, you will remain outside and make sure we spend no more than thirty minutes in there. Use the annunciator at thirty minutes to ring us out, just in case."

Geraldine and DeeDee looked confused.

"The spa is a portal," Ginni said, casually. "I'll tell you more later."

Geraldine and Donovan nodded their heads. What else could they do in a house like this, where the abnormal was just another day.

"Ok," Layce said, "Finally, do you want me to tell you now about the guy's head that fell off?"

Everyone looked at Layce and their jaws dropped. She took that as a yes!

Chapter Twenty-Seven
The Door Slammed and His Head Rolled to the Floor

"Excuse me," Jo choked out with coffee lodged in her throat.

Donovan got up and got the coffee pot to give everyone a warm up.

"So, I took them through the halls. It is really scary, Jo, going up there, you know. I was scared myself, but I took them through the halls and into the other rooms until we got to the Cold Room. I opened the door with this one group and of course the door stuck. That was my first sign of trouble. I said under my breath facing the door and away from the guests, 'Open this door', baring my teeth. Magically, it opened. They all came in and I told the story of levitation that Mom had experienced when she came into this room when you were out, against your wishes to stay downstairs, and how you found her, the room in a windstorm with no windows open and her unconscious body levitating in said wind above the bed. People were freaked out and then I said, 'Come along into the Cold Room.' I opened the door to the walk-in closet to explain where we were about to go and when I did that the bedroom door slammed shut and there was a thud on the floor. A purple glass skull head rolled to my feet. I looked

169

up and it was the man with the cane. At that moment the handle of his cane just happened to pop off and roll onto the floor. We were all so scared at the sounds that when we saw it and he ran up to me to get it we all just burst out laughing. They stopped laughing once I started telling them the story of where we were going and what happened in that room. It's very sobering."

"Yes, it is," Jo said. "What is it with me and houses with terrifying closets?"

Layce reached out and touched her sister's hand.

Chapter Twenty-Eight
The Fog

Her parents looked down from the second story window of her room into the garden. Their daughter was in her little white dress, stabbing at the mud in the corner, getting it dirty, lace becoming browned, like decaying flesh. Garden shears in her hand, mutilating the ground with pleasure, stabbing motions that gave a chill to her parents, the onlookers of something that felt off.

Something was wrong and although neither said a word to one another, they were watching with abject fear. Fear for their daughter, of course, who she was, who she would become, but also for themselves. She had an unmistakable, diabolical nature that at such a young age was puzzling and in certain moments even caused them to fear for their own safety. Neither discussed it but felt the coldness of their own daughter's presence.

A closeup of a doll hanging from a child's hand, two walking, both children, one a toddler, the other a child herself. Walking feet, the clatter of shoes on the pavement, the toddler, a baby just taken out of her backyard shielded by only landscape gates, Italian cypresses and a clear pathway through them. Ada played a game with the toddler. Hide in the trees.

171

"Found you." Ada said on the outside of the cypresses, the side not in the yard of the house, exposed to windows." Let's play at my house."

Innocence understands no fear. The child took the toddler's hand. Walking between bushes and over flower beds. Suddenly in her own garden with a child ready to have fun, and the hand she holds is no child, but a demon wrapped in a child's body. The toddler, a babe to badness.

No people lingering, empty halls, a clear pathway up the front stairs, avoid the servants back staircase. *Mother will be taking tea in the library.* Entering the back of the house and in total silence they would clear the front with no one seeing.

"We must be completely silent, okay?" the monster said with the smile of a child. Only an adult would read the sinister hiding in that smile.

The toddler only nodded yes, seeming now a little afraid. Even she understood in her gut something was wrong.

The house watched as Ada walked down the luxurious hall, passed the servants' station, and into her room. The door closed behind them, the little girl, holding her doll. For the child, the door closed forever. She had no idea it was her final journey, and the fun and games was not the kind she had imagined.

Sufani Weisman-Garza

"Jo," Layce called out.

Jo snapped awake, standing inside the Cold Room, the monsters kill room, the same window she had just seen her parents look out of into the garden, knowing something was wrong with their child. Jo was fuzzy and it took her a moment to come to. She was standing looking out that same window.

Layce came up to her slowly and looked at her face. "Jo? Are you alright? What's going on? Why are you in here?"

Jo was discombobulated and couldn't speak.

"Come on, sis. Let's get you out of here and downstairs," Layce said and ushered her down the hall, through the hole in the wall, into the bedroom and out the door into the hallway. The Cold Room door was closed.

As they walked down the hall, Jo began to become more consciously awake. The daydream state, the vision haze, was lifting.

"I want to go into the cottage," she said, relying on her sister's compassion to escort her out. She took her down the servants' stairs, passing Ginni and Geraldine in the kitchen. She gently held her arm escorting her as her fog was lifting.

"What's going on?" Ginni said.

173

Layce did not answer. Ginni and Geraldine just followed behind. They all exited the house.

One point for the monster.

Chapter Twenty-Nine
Trance of Terror

Sitting in the cottage comfortably, tea was poured. They all sat around Jo in the living room as she collected herself.

"Take a sip of tea," Layce said, concerned.

Jo did as she was told. They sat in the comfort of her beautiful cottage, safe, but from what? None of them knew what had just happened.

"What happened, dear?" Geraldine said compassionately.

Silence filled the room. They were giving Jo the time she needed.

"She wanted me to see it. Well, I'm not sure whose eyes I was seeing it through. Maybe the house's ... yes, I think it was the house showing me ... I don't know. I'm not sure," she said in a daze and babbling.

"Jo!" Layce said sharply. "Snap out of it!" and just then, she did.

"Thank you, sis." She smiled and looked around at everyone there. "That was so weird."

Ginni asked gently, "Why were you in the Cold Room? You know no one is allowed in there on their own. Your rules." Ginni was a protector and was defensive for her friend, almost sister-in-law and now boss.

"I have no memory of going there. That's scary," she said. "You and I had worked on the set-up for the gift shop, I left you and Layce there together going over ideas and was going to check in on you in a while. I sat in the kitchen at the table adjusting the tour schedule and making the tours and stay live on the website, and the next thing I know, I'm in the Cold Room and Layce, you were waking me up."

"Were you sleep walking then? Did you fall asleep at the table you were working at?" Layce asked.

"No, this was no sleep walking. It was like a trance. A trance of terror. I saw it, how it all began," Jo said in a dreamy kind of way that was chilling to the group. They felt the dread of her experience.

The group waited for her as she took a sip. Jo continued.

"I saw how it all began." She paused and took another sip. The group remained silent and let Jo take her time.

"At first, I saw the parents looking out of her bedroom window," Jo looked at them. "The one we now know as the Cold Room." She paused again, clearly seeing it in her mind.

"Oh, boy," Geraldine said with a tone of worry for what she might hear.

"They were watching her from the window. She was in the garden in a white lace dress and had garden shears or something like that and as they watched her, she was just gleefully stabbing the mud."

Layce's back tightened as she gasped, causing her to sit more upright, as she covered her mouth.

Jo continued, "Her dress was getting filthy with dirt. But the parents were not concerned with that. It was like they knew their daughter was something else … evil. They were even scared of her, it felt like," she said, looking at the group. "They knew something was wrong with her. But what were they to do? "

"They had to have felt something from their own child, like something was wrong with her or … just off. Poor parents. I couldn't imagine being in that situation," Layce said feeling compassion for the parents.

Then I saw how she did it. I think it may have been her first abduction. She played games with them, and she always knew how to manipulate them because they were so innocent. Hide and Seek. She would tell them to hide in the perimeter bushes of their houses to get them to be in a place where she could take them out the other side and they walked all by themselves to a hiding place, and then to the house. She would tell them, *Let's play at my house*, and they innocently would go with her. She held their

177

hands. Child to child, they were just playing a game. And she was aware of the servants in the house and where everyone would be to go in the house unnoticed. The parents were in the library having tea and she entered from the back so she could not be seen going up the front steps from the library. Geraldine, just like you didn't see me in a trance going up there. You were in the library putting together the house history book. Right?"

"Yes, dear, just like we discussed," Geraldine answered.

"She was aware of the servants and what they were doing, where they were, where her parents were and how-to walk-up stairs with that toddler unseen."

"Oh, no, that's too much, "Layce said, putting her head in her hands. Layce would surely have nightmares from this, as sensitive as she was, thinking about the actual story. Before it had been a fuzzy story, and now it had become clarified and more real.

"Jo, do you think you saw what actually happened?" Ginni asked in disbelief.

Jo simply nodded yes.

They all sipped their tea, spooked.

"I saw the final journey that child took! I think the house wanted me to see it."

"You didn't see …?" Layce's voice dropped off.

"No, thank God! I didn't see that!"

Jo had always had the power of sight. Sometimes she didn't want it, but at times in her life it came. She never knew what to do with it. It didn't have much place in her corporate life. But she was about a million miles away from corporate nonsense and was in the eye of the psychic storm.

"This was a trance of terror. I feel like the house itself wanted me to see what happened." She set her tea cup down and put two fingers over her mouth staring out her window into the beautiful garden, the absolute contrast to the nightmare she just witnessed. The same garden that had a tiny corner where the monster once stabbed at the mud, practicing her murderous delights.

"Layce will you …?"

"Yes," Layce responded. "I'm not letting you sleep here alone tonight."

"Can I …?"

"Yes," Jo said to Ginni. "Of course, you can stay too."

Not wanting to leave Geraldine out Jo said, "Geraldine you're wel…" before she could finish her statement Geraldine cut in.

"Oh, hell to the no, dear, but thank you for asking," she said, so nana-like. They all burst out laughing at this funny and so sweet golden girl they were all becoming fast friends with and so fond of.

The bonds forming were the juxtaposition of this strange house. Although the carnage was inside telling its story, it was also bringing a closeness and healing that was to be celebrated. An oxymoron of sorts. It was always amazing to Jo how love and horror could be so cleverly intertwined. Perhaps she finally understood the yin and yang, polar opposites in a circle of fate, the good and bad energy all sort of moving in a circle and hanging on to each other, experiencing it all in a circle of life.

Moving on Jo said, "Let me show you the website and the schedule and what I have done. We can peek and see if there have been any bookings," she said to the group, and they got up and walked to her cottage computer that was always on.

She clicked on the website and there it was, nothing was live.

"What?" Jo said. "That little…" She fiercely went back into it with the girls huddled around her chair behind her as she hit the save button making all the tours and B&B live for next week. She sat back with a smile of victory.

Her angels were over her shoulder, smiling and they all looked at each other. Despite the horrific

180

experience she just had, they still moved forward. There was power in numbers and their support of one another.

Just then her email pinged!

"Oh My God," Jo exclaimed. The group looked on.

GRIMM Night DETECTIVE

She opened the email.

"YES. We'd LOVE to come! Tell us what dates you have available. We need the house to ourselves for at least one night," was all it said.

"Oh, my God," Layce said. They have over a million followers internationally!" and looked at the group.

They all knew right then and there, this thing was gonna blow up, and fast! Opening day, 3/13 was soon approaching.

"I'm gonna message them right now," Jo said and began right then and there in front of the group still standing over her chair in excitement.

Reply:

"Wonderful!!! Pick any Saturday night you want, and we'll book it. Give me a couple of dates as the bookings just went live!
Jo

Send.

Immediately she got a ping:

GRIMM Night DETECTIVE
"How about next weekend, we had a cancellation?"

She opened her calendar slightly alarmed to see it already fuller than she expected. It was good but jarring to see the interest.

"Oh, my gosh," Layce cried out and then smiled excitedly jumping up and down.

Strangely, the Saturday they requested was open still, so she blocked it off quickly on the calendar for them only. They would have all day Saturday and overnight. Bookings on Sunday would resume.

"Kismet," Geraldine whispered.

"We could be the next Shining," Layce exclaimed excitedly.

"The Shining isn't a real place, Layce," Ginni said sarcastically with a giggle.

"I know, but you know what I mean?" She was still buzzing in her body with excitement like a little kid.

Everyone smiled at her enthusiasm.

Reply:

"Done. See you then. You can come any time after 11am on Saturday. You'll have the whole house to yourself, but I suspect you'll spend a good amount of time in the Cold Room. If you want to go into the spa out back, which I recommend for reasons I can explain when you get here, you need to let me know. It's for your protection I say this. See you soon!

PS, you'll need to sign the waiver like everyone else, just in case, you know?

Love Jo

Send

A quick ding came back.

GRIMM Night DETECTIVE

"Done. See you soon! We'll be there at 11am to talk to you, get some details from you and collect the keys we will need. After that, we'll be on our own please.

Stay Spooky,
Weathers & Maitland

Jo replied, "Done! See you then!"
Send

"Wow, and just like that, we have International YouTubers coming to stay in our B&B," Jo said, sitting back on her chair trying to catch up with her reality. She refreshed the calendar, "Oh my God!!!! The entire first week of tours and B&B is booked solid."

Their eyes bulged in amazement.

"I can't fucking believe this! Sorry Geraldine!" Jo said. Her arms were chilled with hair standing on end. "This is really happening," she said in disbelief.

Geraldine was unfazed by the language. Heads bobbed in amazement.

"No sleep for the wicked!" Jo said and paused. "Let that sink in…"

Chapter Thirty
The Deepest Thoughts

Jo woke up the next morning, got out of her bed and went into the small kitchen, stepped across the large floor rug with her comfortable slippers until she reached the counter and made a kurig one cup coffee and brought it back into bed. Ginni and Layce who stayed the night were still asleep in what would be Layce's room, formerly. She had decided that she, Layce, and her mother when she visited, would each officially stay in the cottage house so she could use the entire house for the tours and BnB. It was safer that way. The dogs didn't move. It was still early, and dark with the sun just starting to come up. She carefully nestled back into bed with her coffee, pulling her soft duvet comforter up around her waist and grabbed the new journal on her side table she bought at a local mystic shop she had discovered while out running errands. These moments were so precious. The world was barely awake and there was something about the space between silence and the movement of life that she cherished.

It was raining outside, nothing new to the Pacific Northwest, and the soft beating of the rain on the roof and her windows was soothing. Things were moving so fast in her life. It was so exciting, even with this new

185

endeavor of tours and a BnB, famous YouTubers coming to stay…it was a lot to take in. There was nothing else to do but move forward, but sometimes she worried it was too fast. The grayness of the outside world and the comfort of her white sheets, loveliness of the glow of her salt lamp and the light only just coming up from outside, surrounded by the cutest and most ridiculous dogs that snore and fart, that made her feel safe. The room, with hanging plants from the ceiling, a soft rug beneath her bed, a white velvet chair in the corner with a fluffy pillow and throw, and a few pieces of art on the walls placed amongst a simple floral wall paper pattern with blush and cream-colored roses, delicate green leaves and small white flowers made the room comfortable and fresh. Wallpaper made everything more beautiful.

Although she was a rock of persistence and endurance, these moments allowed her to feel. Clay has been gone for only five months now, October he died, and now in March a whole new life is beginning without him. So much had happened without him. The thought of that pierced her heart and she took a deep cleansing breath to let herself feel it. She drew a ragged breath like a child who has cried too hard and long. She had been so busy with life's activities, friendships, the house, the yurt, the ideas, that she was able to get a reprieve from her constant grief.

Life was moving fast ahead, but Clay was gone. The pain of that thought hit her and her eyes watered as she opened her journal. She reached over to pick up the book light, attaching it to the journal and then the pen. She opened the book and began to write. She hadn't journaled for a long time, but she felt like she needed to now. She was drawn to it like it would help her empty out her pain, still lingering inside behind her bravery.

Jo's Journal Entry

I'm sitting in this room, it's lovely, and I wish you could see it, Clay. But I suppose if you were still alive, we would never be in this house. We would still be home, and I would be working my marketing job and you would be working your financial job and we would be busy working away. With all this tragedy, I started wondering if we were really living or were we just surviving?

I wish you and I could have shared this life together. Gig Harbor is so beautiful, and the life is a change of pace. Still by water, but somehow different. Because of all the rain, it makes you think more in harmony around nature. These trees everywhere do something to you, they calm you in a way that makes

187

you want to live a more authentic life, a slower life where you appreciate things.

I'm opening a BnB. You would be happy; I can hear you say it is a good investment and way to use the new home. You would love it that I am able to be home and work at the same time. Although I think you would approve of this all, I don't think it is something we would ever have done together. That makes me a little sad. I don't know why. I think you realize how much you aren't living, when something like this happens, when there is loss. I miss you. I am heartbroken but I don't show it. I have developed so many friends here and the community is so welcoming to me, that would make you happy. You would not be happy with the tragedy of this house and the darkness that resides, even still, inside it. When frightening things happen I know you would try to protect me. But you left me alone, Clay, and now I have to protect myself. Part of me is angry at you, part of me is so sad that you suffered your feelings alone and never let me be there for you. I am sad you didn't let me in. But I know you loved me. I try to stay focused on that.

I didn't know that I was gonna write a letter to you. I just thought I would write my feelings out, I felt

188

something stirring in me that I had to write down. I didn't really know what, exactly. Maybe I'll write you more letters? We'll see. Anyway, I feel better. I love you Clay, even across the veil. I love you. Jo
End Journal Entry

Jo heard the sounds of the girls up and in the kitchen. They had a lot of work today to do with the gift shop, food discussions and wrapping up loose ends with work and getting ready for the Grand Opening. Time to get ready. She jumped out of bed.

Chapter Thirty-One
Slight Trepidation

The week ahead consisted of planning, planning every single detail. Layce made her room her own and officially began staying there more often, although she still stayed with Ginni a lot. Jo busily made her mother's room the pinnacle of beauty bringing some pieces up from the basement of the big house, one even being a canopy bed, with the mahogany wood so beautifully preserved all she needed to do was put a good shine on it. She had asked Hank and Moody, the neighbors from across the street to help move some items from the basement to the cottage and they were very agreeable. She insisted on paying them and as it stood, it looked like Moody's electrical knowledge would be an asset to her budding business, and Hank confirmed she would work the gift shop the evenings of the tours. It was all coming together. Before the official opening, however, she needed her mother's room to be set and ready so she could put all her focus on the business and be ready for Lorna to come any time she wanted.

The room stood ready, with new gold velvet curtains hanging on the canopy, a gorgeous antique piece she thought her mother would really appreciate and enjoy. A new large oriental rug was purchased that covered

190

almost the entire floor of the room in the same colors of the wallpaper that ran throughout most of the cottage, gold, cream, blush and fern green. Big comfortable pillows to sleep on, fluffy throw pillows that created an air of softness, a vanity table to put on her makeup, a small writing desk and chair placed by the rooms window and an elegant white tufted bedroom bench placed at the foot of her bed so she could sit while putting on her shoes and clothes. All pieces of furniture were used from the basement with the exception of the bench, that was purchased specially. The furniture belonged to the house, and it felt right they were reinstated to use in the cottage.

Jo loved her mother very much and only wanted her comfortable to stay as long as she liked. She wouldn't mind if her mother stayed indefinitely, but Lorna was *very* independent. It was a quality she appreciated. If Lorna stayed, it would be at her own recommendation and insistence. She was enjoying her life right now and Jo didn't want to interfere with any of her joyous plans. Her door was open anytime Lorna wanted to come to stay or even move in.

Now that Lorna's room and the cottage was officially ready, with occupants already comfortably living in it (she, Layce, and sometimes Ginni), she had a few more days before Weathers and Maitland from Grimm Night

Detective arrived. She would spend that time making sure all the employees knew their schedule, how to clock in and out on the app, etc. Everyone had already signed the waivers, received their offer letters and signed them. Even with family she was taking no chances on clear agreements. Everyone knew what their pay was, hours to begin with that may flex if agreed upon, and things were on track.

She watched the calendar book out and she had many conversations with Ginni already regarding the flow of food to be available for the expanded Continental Plus breakfast each morning, and they also agreed to have all day self-serve coffee and tea, with cookies and scones available at any time of the day. Jo herself had visited a BnB with Clay once that offered this same set-up, a stainless-steel coffee carafe for self-serve coffee and tea, and she loved the idea of self-serve treats in big glass domed antique cake plates, convenient for a guest's schedule, also encouraging them to sit in the downstairs rooms to enjoy the house. Plus, who wouldn't like free treats when they are tasty?

The only thing she would do when her mother came would be to cut fresh flowers from the garden and place them in her room.

Looking over Lorna's room once more, she was pleased with what she had created, called the dogs who

192

were resting comfortably on the rug in Lorna's room and they came to her feet and shuffled out. She shut the door quietly and smiled at her work.

"Well, let's go into the big house and do a walkthrough," she said to the dogs. They seemed happy to oblige at this moment, perhaps knowing they would only be asked to follow downstairs. English bulldogs who are built like walking tabletops don't do stairs well. It was a mutual agreement that Jo would mostly leave them downstairs when she ventured upstairs, and they seemed more than fine with that arrangement. If they chose to come, it was up to them.

They all walked out of the cottage headed towards the big house. The rain had stopped, and beams of sun were peeking out here and there from behind the clouds. She admired the new landscaping of the cottage, the path created recently with flowers and ferns budding up against the cobble stone walkway overflowing with volume and color. Geraniums in all the colors were blossoming as they do all year round. The hydrangea bushes up against the cottage house were full and bushy, with the flowers just beginning their spring appearance, with ferns taking to the soil and growing to monstrous size, just as she had hoped. Ferns grew wild in the Pacific Northwest and flourished, and she wanted them everywhere.

193

She and Clay had an apartment together before they were married and owned the condo and they had had two ferns on their lovely back patio. She remembered when they moved out and Clay gently took one of the ferns from its spot to move into the moving truck, and it had grown well out beyond the perimeter of the patio fence. As he began separating it from its home it had been in for years, it was as if it had woken up and its slumped over body sat upright and grew to twice its size. She remembered how surprised Clay was and said it grew like a monster putting up both of its arms like a zombie reaching out for him and the fence. Its leaves became its clutching hands. The ferns loved their home there and she always felt bad that they did not take to the new place and died shortly after, as much as she tried to save them.

She used to sit out on her patio and watch the plants, studying them, after reading, *The Secret Life of Plants*. She watched as each separate plant would turn their face toward the sun no matter what position she put them in, that they would reach out and touch each other and create a support network. She even realized later that, when plants and trees are in the ground, they do the same thing, reaching out to all other trees and plants so that when one tree is not getting what it needs, it creates a root system to try to help nourish it. Nature creates a whole

194

underground network of support, and it fascinated her. Ever since then, plants, flowers, trees and nature were magical to her. She realized we needed them more than they needed us. If the world ended, they would survive beyond humanity. She had a deep love and respect for nature and the will to live.

The white picket fence created around the cottage made it feel separate and like a home and she and the dogs loved the new setup. It was strange how it all ended up, and yet she felt comfortable there in the cottage, as if it were all meant to be. They crossed the barrier of their cottage boundary, turned right to the walkway to the house and headed up the stairs to the big house, the Purdy House. The dogs managed the stairs this day. Some days were easier than others and she helped them as needed. Every move they made and stair they hurdled was accompanied by a snort, the sound of a collar shaking, or general noises of effort being made, followed by her encouragement, "You all did so good! Nice job. I know that wasn't easy for you," she said leaning down to talk to them, touching and patting them lovingly, and they ate it up. They were meant to be loved!

She put the key into the back door of the house and turned the knob. It jammed.

Sufani Weisman-Garza

"Mother Fuc***," she turned the knob again and it opened.

Nuclear curse words aborted.

They all crossed the threshold and entered the Purdy House, as always, with slight trepidation.

Chapter Thirty-Two
The Walk-Through

"*Hello,*" she announced as the dogs rushed in and went directly into the kitchen sniffing around for loose morsels.

"Why did I do that," she asked herself, knowing she was the only one in the house. She was slightly creeped out that she did that because she knew who was in the house and she did not want to have an interaction with it, with her. She exhaled deeply. "That was stupid." Already she felt she had woken something up and had a "feeling". She looked at the dogs and they were fine, so she carried on. The dogs had always been a trusted bellwether.

"Ok, kiddos, let's begin the walk-through and check every room," she said to them, mostly because it calmed her own nerves that had just begun to be unsettled. Somehow, talking to the dogs about what she was doing made her feel better.

She had learned not to put her keys down on the kitchen counter or island because they may not be there later. When she first moved in, she had placed her keys down in one place and when she returned, they were in another. She tucked them into the back pocket of her jeans which was now bulging.

There were two bedrooms and two bathrooms downstairs so she would begin her walk-through with them. She began with what was her mother's room before all the incidents with the house and even with Lorna. She entered Lorna's old *room* that was a large bedroom. It was the downstairs suite with a full bath and a gorgeous claw foot bathtub, rose colored velvet wallpaper in its traditional antique designed style. Jo had made this room even more gorgeous by placing all the things her mother would need to be comfortable, much as she had done again for her in the cottage house. A vanity table, a small writing desk, a black rotary phone that worked, a plush rug beneath the bed that took up almost the entire room with the hardwood visible where the rug did not cover. A side table on either side of her bed, faux floral arrangements and fake hanging ferns and palm tree in the corner because Jo just didn't see how she would have time to take care of all the plants in a home this size, although she planned on taking time here and there to add fresh in the rooms when it made sense and always inside the house and common areas for the guests. She would blend the two, real and unreal, and guests may be none the wiser. She loved well-made fake plants and trees because they kept a lovely look all year long. They only needed cleaning which she would build into the process. Eventually she had planned on

198

naming all the rooms specifically, but at this point they were only numbered, with the exception of the Cold Room. This room was gorgeous like the rest of the house with gold velvet wallpaper and the natural green bringing in the feeling of the outdoors, indoors in that Pacific Northwest style.

The dogs seemed to still smell Lorna, who they loved, and were sniffing around as she made sure everything was in perfect place to receive their first guest in just a few days. It was perfect and so she moved on and did the same in the second bedroom which was not a suite but quite nice. The bathroom was just outside the bedroom door and also would be used as a bathroom for all guests who lingered in the common areas. That bathroom would be spotless at all times. Jo couldn't stand dirty bathrooms or fingerprint smudges on glass doors, or mirrors, especially in public places; or handles; all handles must be cleaned daily with so many people coming and going. Fingerprints everywhere just showed a lack of care as well as being disgusting. It would be cleaned continually, and she would make a note to hire someone to come in regularly. Perhaps she would even hire someone to just keep the house and cottage clean daily on staff. With the schedule booked as it would, she could afford to do it. She made a mental note.

199

She turned to look at the back staircase and looked up before taking a step. "Ok, let's do it," and she began the ascent of the staircase. She looked back to see the dogs hesitate for a second and then joyfully began to push their heavy bodies up the stairs one at a time and continually look up at her to see how much further they had to go. Nos even took a seat on a stair giving himself a little break. "Ok, I'll meet you guys up here. I have to get busy," she said, looking back at them as she reached the top of the stairs and onto the second floor.

She couldn't help but feel a chill and a slight uneasiness being up there. The memory of being thrown and slapped by an unseen force always lingered in her mind. She had no choice but to be brave, but that did not mean she wasn't terrified inside. The beauty of the house always betrayed the potential for violence and her instincts were already on alert. She began by tending to the large closet closest to the back staircase on the back wall. It had clearly been a maids' area where the servants could come up the backstairs and use the main closet for all their supplies. There was also a laundry chute, which was so creepy, that ended in the basement where the washer and dryer were, amongst other items like furniture, draperies, photos and personal items of the home. There were places in the basement below that were so black under the house that she did her best to forget it existed. It was a terrifying space and although at some point she would need to investigate it, right now she focused on the part of the house she could manage. Just thinking of the darkness beyond the washer, dryer and general storage area creeped her out. Only God knew what was down there in the deep darkness. She had considered once going down there with a candle and quickly changed her mind when the lone candle light seemed to be eaten up by the darkness. She hadn't yet gone back, but knew she would sometime soon, but not alone and with many lights. It was a scary place.

What was also scary was what she now knew to be an added closet that purposely distorted the fact that there was a room off the staircase behind the railing at one time. It had been cleverly hidden with the immense closet structure made to look like original, as it looked just like the closets in the bedroom. They were well crafted in hardwood, ornate woodworking, and so beautiful it could only be seen as art. They were deeper than they looked from the outside because by some amazing architecture strategy, some optical illusion, they were placed in corners or offset in ways, like this one, that fooled the eyes. The closet behind the railing looked simply like a large and gorgeous servants' closet. But in actuality, it hid the room

201

that was once Ada's, now only accessible by a hole in the closet in the Cold Room. The trees outside, so heavy in brush, and tall thick Italian trees, mixed with the angles of the house cleverly hid the depth of the hidden room. So many tricks of the eye were used inside and outside. No one ever noticed the hidden room from the inside or out. Jo had no intention of changing it either. It would simply now be a part of the history of the house. At least this way she felt evil was contained, although she knew very well it was not.

There was a simpler closet to the left of the staircase upon coming up to the landing on the second floor and this would have been more realistic as the original closet for servants to use. It was obvious by the woodwork and effort that it was less ornate and set back. She thought how clever it was to keep people from seeing something by making them look at it but making them see something completely different, making them see what you wanted them to see. The room was hidden in plain sight the whole time, as intended. Although back in the nineteenth and early twentieth centuries, no guests would have ever ventured up those stairs per etiquette and custom. Perhaps they were thinking of the future, or simply the servants?

202

The velvet mauve and gold wallpaper that ran the expanse of the upstairs was so beautiful it always took her breath away. The floor rugs that ran the space of the hall were antiques themselves and had been well preserved. She opened the closets now used for supplies and checked that all the towels, soaps and things the guests' rooms would need to be supplied with for every turn of the room were present. The closets were in perfect condition and well supplied, so she turned to move down the hall. The hall stretched out like a psycho movie, and she inched her way down it and went into the first room on the right. All the rooms now had Jo's touch, perfect placement of a vanity, writing desk, end tables, and rotary phone, There was one phone line that all phones were connected to, and she believed most would find it more novelty than necessity, since everyone had cellphones these days. Many today don't even know how to use a rotary phone. There are many videos on YouTube of adults watching their kids try to figure out how they worked that she found funny. But in a pinch, lights out, or Wi-Fi outage, it was nice to know that in such a large property, there was landline out.

She checked the cabinets and dressers drawers to make sure all was clear or stocked and the towels were hanging with extra towels in the bathroom. She checked the fireplace and that the flue was open since this time of

203

Sufani Weisman-Garza

year people may want a fire in their room. Extra firewood was placed by every room's fireplace with burning kindling and a long neck lighter for convenience. Every room also had an installed fire extinguisher hanging low on the wall by the fireplace, and candles in the rooms were all on a timer so as not to encourage other flames than the fireplace. Two candle wall candelabras were electric and plugged in, but looked exactly like flickering candles for effect and were placed in all the rooms for ambiance. The fireplace mantle had antique pictures found in the basement and other accoutrement from the home's history for décor. Every room was gorgeous but also not overdone.

She left that room and entered back down the hall to her old room on the right, right across from the Cold Room. She had a way of passing it and acting as though it was not there, but as she passed it the hair on her body stood on end like electricity that she could not deny. If her mind was avoiding acknowledging the room, her body never could. She walked past it and into her old room which was now to be another guest room directly across from the infamous Cold Room. So far, her room had always been a sort of safe place from any happenings, although not safe from wicked dreams, foreshadowing events and messages from ghosts. For some reason, the

204

room had seemed to be a safe haven from the girl. It had been thus far, but Jo trusted nothing to be true long term in this house. It felt more homey in her old room, perhaps more than that, almost trapped in time, but somehow also present. It was welcoming to her and held its own authority and perhaps, she wondered, it may have been the room of the girl's parents. She would never know for sure, but she assumed so. For what other reason would the girl avoid that room, even in death?

She checked the fireplace and the fire extinguisher; she checked the bathroom supplies and the locks on the windows. She looked down below from the bay window facing the front of the house to see the huge tree getting fuller every day while remembering that first day she moved in and saw the bones of its features in winter. Each branch had looked like long wicked fingers reaching out to people on the street and also to the house. It was spooky then and was still so now that it was in bloom. The trees were complicit in hiding the house's secrets by no fault of their own. Even the plot seemed aware of itself, knowing that it shields a haunted house of horrors. Land held energy from events, she knew that from her Native American Heritage and empathic nature. Events could and do leave a stain not only on people, but on land too. The land was aware of what happened here, just as Clay's death

Sufani Weisman-Garza

would leave a stain, a haunting, on that closet he hanged dead in. The one she ran from.

As she finalized plumping pillows and giving it a last look through, she stalled, knowing her next look would be into the Cold Room Suite, but she would not be entering the Cold Room itself, the backroom of horror. She would not enter the closet, that led to the hole in the closet, that led to a long dark dilapidated hallways with wallpaper peeling off life skin, into the room where many children took their last breath and had horrific things done to them, hopefully after they were already dead.

As she looked at the door of the Cold Room from the safety of her room – the Safe Room, perhaps that is what she would call it when she named all the rooms – the door was just a normal door like all the rest of the rooms, but it felt as though it was breathing, taking in breaths as though it had a chest and lungs. Was it her imagination? She thought so. Her heart began to beat a little faster. She felt heat rise to her neck and could feel her face flush red with blood. The door, a normal door, was menacing just the same, and she needed to open it to check the room. Although she had decided she would only rent this room out to certain people, perhaps those interested in investigating, she would not allow just anyone to sleep in it as it was connected to that horrible room, the kill room, connected to the cold room suite through the hole in the closet.

She stepped out of her old room having finished her walk-through of it, and turned to take a final look, turning her back to the Cold Room. She was pleased with what she saw. It was ready. As she turned back around to face the Cold Room door, she saw something from the corner of her eye peek out from the bathroom area wall in the shadows. It was not a shadow but a full apparition in white, for just a moment and then it was gone. It startled her for a moment, but she wasn't afraid, it was familiar. She had seen this before. Ada's mother, the Lady in White, as she had called her, was still watching. She had thought she was gone. She had seen the girl's parents leave when the horrible truth of the Cold Room was discovered. Once the truth was known, they were released. Just like all those children's spirits trapped inside this house of horrors. Perhaps a mother's love knows no bounds and if her daughter was still here, then she had decided to remain. She had protected Jo from her in the past by throwing her physically away from the room where the girl was, by giving her clues in her dreams, whispering things in her ears to help her discover the truth. Jo didn't know how it all worked beyond the veil, but she was relieved nonetheless. The mother, whom she had thought was an adversary, in

207

the end was only trying to help her see what danger was in the house when all the original happenings occurred there.

She turned back to look in the Safe Room hoping to see her again.

"Is that you Mrs. Purdy?"

There was sonly silence. Nothing materialized. Her heart, although comforted by her sighting of the mother who was an ally to her, made her feel no better about opening that door. For if the mother was there, danger lurked.

"Okay," she said out loud, turning around and stepped up to the Cold Room door and twisted the handle. The door opened. A sweet smell of lavender from the potpourri entered her nostrils as the door remained only cracked for her to see the grey of the day filtering minimal light into the room. The trees were in bloom and looked lovely outside the room, but it was all a façade for what lay inside. As the door began to swing more open, she began to turn her gaze to the left of the room toward the closet and bathroom area and was surprised to see Layce standing there facing a closed closet in the dark shadows of the room.

"Layce?"

No answer.

The hair on Jo's arms stood on end.

"Layce?" she said again louder. Layce's body began to twitch in strange jerky movements, her neck contorting her head in strange ways. Jo was petrified but had had enough of this room and lunged toward her sister to snap her out of whatever spell she was under and drag her out of this Godforsaken room. The room had a grip on her sister as it did with her mother's incident with the room.

"Layce," she yelled, terrified, but still grabbed her arm. The most terrible screeching scream came out of the face that turned to look at her. It looked like Layce rotting, with messy hair, dark holes for eyes, and a contorted mouth too wide and long for its face, screaming so loud at her that her ears popped in pain. She let go and grabbed her ears. The screaming sound seemed to be coming out from every orifice of the house. It was followed by a sort of metal grinding sound that was unnatural. She backed up quickly in shock and out of the room faster than she could humanly have thought and the thing screaming was still facing her as it slammed the door in her face as she tripped and fell backwards to the floor in the hallway. It was when she fell that she realized there were no dogs. Even while falling, she worried she might fall on them, but there were no dogs. They never came up. She scrambled and picked herself up and ran to the back staircase and as she did something snatched the back of her neck and pulled hard. Here eyes bulged in terror.

"Jo. ... *Jo!*" Layce yelled clutching her shoulder near her neck to shake her.

Just then Jo twitched hard and let out a horrified scream and looked up to see Layce's face above her.

"Jo? Jo, what's wrong. Are you okay?" Layce asked very concerned. Jo was breathing very heavily and perspiring freely and did not answer, but simply looked around.

Gold, blush and cream roses, ferns, small white flowered wallpaper. She was in her room. She was in her bed. She looked to her end table. Her coffee cup was empty, and the pen was on the side table. She looked down at herself; she was in her pajamas with the journal laying across her chest, still lying in bed, the dogs now in the other room once Lacye opened the door to her room.

"Jo, wake up! Are you alright, Sis?"

Jo, clearly not, was drenched in sweat. Disoriented, she sat up in her bed and looked around. "What day is this, what time is it?"

A look of real worry came over Layce's face and her brow furrowed with confusion. "Jo, it's Thursday, Sis. Are you okay?" She was softly rubbing her sister's arm now, consoling her.

Jo was completely disoriented and asked for a glass of water. As Layce went out of the room she looked down at her journal and it was what she had journaled that morning. She must have fallen back asleep and had that nightmare. Was it a nightmare? It was like living a full day. It was so real. Layce came back into her room and sat on the bed next to her, giving her the water. Jo drank the whole glass.

"Come on, let's get you out of this bed."

"I need a shower," Jo said, as her PJs stuck to her body, and she wiped her wet face.

As she held Jo's arm for reassurance and walked her to her shower Layce asked, "What happened Jo?"

"The Lady In White…she's still in the house Layce?"

Layce said nothing. She listened intently, getting Jo a fresh towel and turning on the water for her.

"Well, that's not so bad, is it?" she asked. "Ultimately, she was helpful, right? She was protecting you?" She began helping her take off her jammies.

"You were in the Cold Room, Lacye." Jo's breath was still ragged from her racing heart. Layce listened and watched her face.

"I was."

"It wasn't you, sister. It was a trick, a mimic of you. I touched you and you became a screeching beast. The girl was pretending to be you," Jo said, assisting in removing her nightclothes and stepping into the shower. There was no modesty between her and Layce. They were sisters.

"What were you doing in the dream?"

"I don't know if it was a dream, Layce."

"Sis, remember I woke you from your bed?" she said, sitting on the closed toilet seat like they did when they were children talking to each other in the shower.

Jo plunged her bed head and sweaty face in the water, and it brought her back from her stupor, slowly. "I think it was a foreshadowing or message."

"What were you doing?" Layce asked again.

"Layce, I did the whole walk through, just like we are scheduled to do today. I will be able to tell you everything that will need to be done before I even enter that house," and she proceeded to tell her from the dogs behavior to each room and closet she checked.

Layce got a chill knowing the girl was now mimicking people. Next time, Jo would not do the walk through alone.

After a reset, it was time to do the walk through. Ginni had left a long time ago for the café. It was just Jo, Layce and the dogs now. Power in numbers.

212

Jo peeked in at Lorna's room on the way out. Perfectly designed. Everything perfectly placed. She closed the door smiling at her work.

They all walked out of the cottage headed towards the big house. Jo admired the new landscaping of the cottage, the path created recently with flowers and ferns budding up against the cobble stone walkway overflowing with volume and color. Geraniums in all the colors were blossoming.. The hydrangea bushes up against the cottage house were full and bushy, flowers just beginning their spring appearance, with ferns taking to the soil and growing to monstrous size, just as she had hoped. Ferns grew wild in the Pacific Northwest and flourished, and she wanted them everywhere. She and Clay had ferns once!

Chapter Thirty-Three
Grimm Night Detective

One day to the arrival of GND, Grimm Night Detective. She knew absolutely nothing about them and put all her trust in Layce, who did. If Layce said they were important to the haunt community, she believed her, but she now had time to be curious enough to go on YouTube and see who they were. After all, they would be on her doorstep tomorrow morning at eleven and she thought it only prudent to know who would be looking her in the eyes soon enough. She also thought it appropriate to know the level of grit of one Maitland and Weathers. She wanted to make sure they had the sensibility and staying power to make it through the night.

It was early afternoon, and she was inside the cottage and had just made herself a sandwich and brought it to her laptop at her desk to eat and do an investigation of her own. Ginni and Layce were out in the yurt putting the final touches to the gift shop and spa and were working in twos for safety. Hank from across the street, the new gift shop sales-girl was coming for training in an hour or so and Layce was handling that. When they were done there, they would head into the house together to get the kitchen set up for their first guests, GND. Even though they would

214

be the only ones staying that night in the house for their investigation, they would still get the full treatment of Continental Plus Breakfast, coffee, tea, and pastries. The full treatment. They would be allowed to stay in the Cold Room to sleep if they wanted, but Jo intended to have them stay in her old room overnight and have full access to the Cold Room to investigate, or whatever it was they did to report back to their followers.

She typed in Grimm Night Detective. The latest video popped up on the screen and looked intriguing. Their catalog of places they had been to was impressive. Winchester Mystery House, The Warren's Haunted Museum of Demon infested items, famous grave sites, Salem's Haunted museums, Midsummer Scream and every monster and paranormal con imaginable, haunted houses both Halloween and real, famous and even lesser known. They even had made a trip to the Salem Satanic temple and took viewers on their journey through it. Jo found them fascinating and understood why Layce was so excited.

Maitland was a stunning gothic woman. She couldn't be more than five feet two, wore black pants and black jacket in every video but always a colorful shirt beneath. A gothic black webbed necklace, and bright neon yellow hair with bright blood red lipstick, that seemed to be her signature. Her skin was naturally pale and soft like powder and she wore no other makeup on her face other than a small amount of mascara. Her eyes were pale green and added to her spooky yet mesmerizing look. She would often wear a large brim fedora hat in black.

Weathers was equally interesting. He spoke with his long fingers stretched out like knives emphasizing his words hauntingly and theatrically. He loved the macabre, it was obvious. He loved what he did, and it showed in his enthusiasm and need to teach everyone watching what the truth was about each location or experience. He was driven to help everyone watching feel the same experience and then take a journey themselves to that location. Although Maitland was in almost every video, by his side or walking ahead, filming her walk as he talked, in ghost host fashion, Weathers did all the talking to express the experience they were having or going to have and then commenting and questioning it at the end of each video, inviting the viewers to take their own trip to the location to see for themselves. He had long thin jet-black hair, silky and well-kept, large black rimmed Cary Grant-like glasses, and he chose his clothing carefully. Always a simple black t-shirt in the genre of horror or gothic bands, black tight pants and equally gothic shoes. He wore black bracelets on his right arm, and large gothic rings on both hands in silver.

She could only surmise silver, chosen to keep the vampires at bay. His eyes seemed as black as his hair and his skin as pale as Maitland's. Weathers was easily six feet tall and although dark and gothic looking himself, he was very likeable, when he smiled he invited you into his world with friendship. He seemed like a good man who was a dark lord of haunted nerdy goodness. In many videos, when he met someone he worshipped, he would be overcome as a fan, blush and sometimes even seem awkward, although he learned his lines to get back on track. He would lose himself and would leave it in the cut, which only made you like him more.

On occasion he would be wearing a Jazz bolero in black. At the end of each video, they would close with a frame on both their faces as he said, "Till next time… Stay Spooky," and his fingers like daggers would stretch out and poke into the camera on a close up and then fade to black.

She had spent almost ninety minutes watching their videos without realizing it. She hit subscribe. She was now a fan herself and excited that she actually would get to meet them tomorrow. From the videos, they did not seem squeamish or scared easily and had been in scary situations before. She felt secure in the decisions they would make for themselves on whether to stay in the Cold Room or not based on their seasoned experience, although she

217

would encourage them not to sleep in there, but in the Safe Room, her old room, across the hall.

She had eaten her sandwich and sour cream chips and closed her laptop and carried her dish to the sink, rinsed it and put it in the dishwasher. Just then Layce, Ginni and Hank came into the cottage.

Hey," Jo said to everyone walking in. She saw Hank scan the living room and smile.

"So pretty," Hank said and smiled at Jo.

"Awe, thanks, Hank," Jo said, sweetly. "All set for the Sunday crowds."

Hanks eyes widened in excitement and said, "Oh, yes, so excited."

"Jo, we're gonna take Hank inside on a general tour of the place and then make sure the kitchen is all prepped for tomorrow. Sound good?" Layce asked.

Ginni smiled at Jo, equally excited for Grimm Night Detective. "I can't believe GND will be here tomorrow."

"I know, me too. I just got sucked into their videos for ninety minutes," Jo smiled.

"Yah, they're addictive, right?" Layce said, rhetorically. "OK, well, we're heading in. Check on us soon."

"Fill Hank in on the rules of the house please."

"Oh, we have," Layce replied. "Always in pairs, never alone. And even that can't protect you from portals."

Hank's eyes lit up in glee. "I love this shit," she said, giggly. "Doh, is that alright to cuss in front of the boss?" she said to Jo. They all laughed.

"Fuck, yah," Ginni replied and laughed.

Jo smirked. "Yes, but never in front of guests and, well, take it easy, we are still a class act, well, at least we want others to think so," Jo said playfully, and they all laughed as Layce ushered them out the front door of the cottage. They had work to do.

Jo watched them as they took fresh blood into the house and looked up above the door of the back house into that mysterious optical illusion area covered with trees and shrubberies and wondered what she would see if the windows were exposed. She wondered if little demon eyes would peer back at her as she looked in the direction of that secret room. She wondered how long Hank would last, or how much she would still *love this shit,* after she has her own experience? And she would have her own experience. It was only a matter of time.

Chapter Thirty-Four
The Arrival

Jo, Layce, Ginni and their new addition, Hank, were all in the cottage waiting with excitement, and sitting having coffee nervously in the living room, as they heard tires crunching on gravel. Jo noticed Hank toss her long shiny brown hair to her back. Although feminine and beautiful, somewhere in her early forties she surmised, she was not overly girly; the kind that is always fussing with her hair and looks. No muss, no fuss, just like her, and she liked it.

"It's them," Jo said, and they put their coffees down on the coffee table and jumped up.

Jo saw the large SUV that pulled into the drive slowly and saw neon yellow hair in the passenger seat. The SUV had tinted windows, so it was difficult to see them, but the hair was noticeable, even so. The car stopped slowly in front of the big house; they were looking at it, as the car continued to run. All the women watched like Mrs. Kravitz the nosy, peering neighbor in Bewitched, looking through the sheer curtain in the front living room, to see what Grimm Night Detective would do next. After about five seconds, the car continued to roll into the drive toward the back all the way up to the gate where the drive ended and the rest of the spacious garden could be seen,

220

including the cottage house and yurt. The front windows of the cottage had a long view of the drive from where it was positioned.

The car shut off. Two doors opened, driver side and passenger side. From where they were watching, The large gothic skull punk motorcycle boots of Weathers dropped to the gravel one, and then the other, and as he stood they got a look at him.

"Wow," Jo said out loud. "What a presence." Weathers was a tall, toned and thin man, but not gangly, perhaps less focused on muscular bulk than some men. She chalked that up to interest. He didn't strike her as the kind of guy who needed to sit around watching ball games or pumping himself up at the gym. He seemed very into… whatever he was into, Jo thought, that has made him famous; ghost hunting and macabre journeys. His hair was jet black, long and thick, pale white skin, gothic. He wore dark sunglasses even though it was grey outside. She was intrigued.

The group all looked at one another in silent awe. He was YouTube famous and the effect on them was the same as any other celebrity. Jo seemed to be the only one who had not really known about him, them, until recently.

The passenger side door closed, and Maitland came around to the front of the car, dressed in black

221

leggings, similar gothic skull boots, and a neon green shirt that said 'Freddy Forever', a black bat cut jacket, and was as stunning in person as on camera. Her long neon yellow hair, her light eyes and pale white skin made her a stunning sight. She appeared to wear little to no makeup, at least from their distance, with the exception of bright red lipstick. They stood for a minute together taking it all in.

"Give them a minute," Jo said, using a pausing gesture to the girls, keeping them from action toward the door. She then looked away from GND to give instructions.

"Layce and I will go to greet them. I don't want to overwhelm them initially. Once we go out, you guys wait on the doorstep for me to bring them up toward the cottage to introduce you. We want to be fans without acting like it … I guess, is what I'm trying to say," and she smiled at Ginni and Hank. They agreed.

Jo opened the cottage door and saw through the stain glass door their heads turn in their direction. She opened the door and stepped out.

"Hello," Jo said walking out of the cottage with Layce behind as they walked down the path toward them. Ginni and Hank waited on the porch as instructed and watched the interaction.

"Well, hello," Weathers said moving toward Jo and Layce with his large white hand out to shake theirs. Maitland followed behind him and was the quieter one until she had something to say, from the videos she had seen.

Jo came forward first and made eye contact with the two and they all smiled at one another. Jo noticed Maitland's eyes were a beautiful light grey.

"Welcome to The Purdy House, she said and smiled at them while shaking Weathers' hand and then Maitland's. She took them in with her eyes and it seemed like they were used to that sort of thing. They seemed other worldly, and Jo got caught up in their magic for a moment and then snapped out of it.

"This is my sister, Layce."

Layce stepped forward and shook their hands. "I'm a big fan of your work. I was the one who told my sister about you. She's only recently become acquainted with your work but was really excited once she knew who you were and what you do." She Looked at Jo and smiled.

"Absolutely," Jo said. "I am excited to have you here. Let me show you the big house first and then I can show you the rest of the grounds. After that, you'll be on your own, minus the cottage, which is where we live.

223

"Oh, so you don't live in the house?" Weathers asked and looked briefly at Maitland.

"Uh, no, not anymore. There is so much to tell you, but I sense you will want to observe most by yourself. I do just want to show you the layout, where to find the creature comforts while you are here, and just give you some cautionary tales for certain areas. I would not be responsible if I didn't give you a heads up on a few things. The rest will be up to what you ask me or want to know."

"Sounds good," Weathers said, and Maitland smiled.

"Oh, but before we do, let me please introduce you to two others who also work here at Purdy House." She made a gesture to move in her direction and they all followed. Ginni and Hank moved forward to the gate of the cottage where it transitioned beyond the fence into the walkway leading to either the yurt or the big house.

"This is Ginni and Hank. Ginni will head up our catering and hospitality, and Hank will be in charge of our Spook shop." Both the women murmured pleasantries and shook their hands.

"Maitland said to Hank, "I love your name," and smiled.

"Thank you," was the simple reply and Jo continued the conversation.

224

"Well, as you can see the cottage here, this is where Layce and I live and use as my office. "

"Do you have activity in the cottage?" Weathers asked?

"Not as of yet, although in the areas where nothing paranormal seems to take place, sightings or anything, terrible distressing dreams do occur, which still feel like an attack."

Weathers looked at Maitland who pulled out a small notepad from her bat jacket and made a note of it. Perhaps to ask about the dreams in more detail.

"To the left of the cottage you can see the yurt, which is where the day spa services will take place and we made a separate section where in the evening it will be used as a spooky gift shop with some merch people exiting the tours can buy, and of course for the BnB guests as well."

"You mentioned something you needed to fill me in on in the yurt?"

"Yes, It's a portal. Well, something happens in there where time slows or is lost."

They both looked ta Jo inquisitively and silent. They wanted more information.

"We were in there looking around at the finishing touches and we lost time, in a nutshell."

"Yah, hours had passed when it felt like just a few minutes," Ginni added. Weathers and Maitland looked at her and took in the information. Hank was hearing some of this for the first time as well. Jo was hoping she wouldn't get freaked out and quit before she ever got started. She saw her eyes bulge in excitement, not fear, so that was a good sign. Jo smirked at her rection and continued.

"So, what I wanted to tell you regarding the yurt was that because services are a timed thing and this portal, not sure what it is, may happen periodically or all the time, I don't really know yet, I have installed an Annunciator so during services it will flash when services are done on a timer. I will also be aware of the service schedule to check and make sure they are not trapped in some time warp. So, I recommend that when you go in there, just let me know by sending me a text and I can show you how to set the timer and also check in on you when you think you might be done to make sure I can pull you out of it if it happens to you. Like I said, I really don't know how much this will happen, I just know it did happen once and since then we have been in there in pairs and with someone on the outside checking time."

They listened intently and Weathers looked at Maitland intrigued and put his chin in his cupped hands for a moment.

"I love this stuff," Maitland said and smiled, not fearful at all.

Jo smiled back at her. "I just needed you to know that, and the rest is up to you," Jo said. "Shall we continue to the big house?"

"Yes, please," Weathers said.

"I can make some coffee inside if you all would like, for after the tour," Ginni suggested.

"Ooh, that would be great," Maitland responded.

"Yes, ditto," Weathers said interested.

They all began to walk to the big house. Jo left the dogs inside the cottage for now and would ask the girls to stay downstairs while she did the upstairs tour as to allow Weathers and Maitland to sense things without so many other people's energies present.

As they all walked up the stairs and entered the back of the house, Ginni, Layce and Hank splintered off to the left and into the kitchen area.

Jo began with the Grimm Night Detectives. "So, this is an eight bedroom house starting right here, two rooms on the first floor that were more than likely not bedrooms at the time. Most Victorians did not sleep on the first floor. There are six rooms on the top floor, only five are actual rooms, one is the hidden room, the Cold Room.

227

They began to climb the back halls stairs leaving everyone else behind.

"So, this room you call The Cold Room, is it the hidden room then?"

"That's a great question. We probably should distinguish a difference between the two as there is a formal room we call the Cold Room, because it's now like one room, attached through the hole in the wall leading back to the hidden room. We should probably call the formal room the Cold Room Suite and then the hidden room, The Cold Room. But honestly, when we reference them now, and we stare at the door off the hallway, it's just, the Cold Room. The back room has penetrated the room, too, so we just see them as one. Lots of activity happens in both sections."

GND took it all in. They reached the landing upstairs, and she took a moment to explain what they were seeing. It would make more sense to them after they saw the hidden room to understand the smoke and mirrors of hidden space created by the large ornate wall cabinet and the maids' closet covering any sign of the outside window behind it as to not orientate yourself to where you were in the house. The shrubbery outside created more distractions so as to not look too closely and where the walls actually began even the shape of the house

228

in that section. So thick and deep, even in winter, that it would never be noticed. So much garden eye candy with the fountain and the vastness of the property, cottage house and trees in the opposite direction, and now a yurt, to lead the eye away from it. They hadn't even noticed, as others had not noticed for generations.

"Ok, here is where it gets complicated," Jo said.

They all stood at the top of the stairs. Maitland and Weathers were eager to hear what she had to say and couldn't help but let their eyes dart around. Weathers maintained eye contact more directly while Maitland's curiosity showed as she began to touch the wallpaper and woodworking on the staircase and wherever she saw it. Like a kid in a candy store. Jo understood, she had felt the same way when she first came into the house. Jo smiled in her direction. Maitland turned and focused her attention to the end of the hallway on the left. Jo already knew Maitland felt it as a clairvoyant.

"Ahem." Weathers sounded, falsely clearing his throat only to catch Maitland's attention to focus on her story telling.

"Oh, I'm sorry, Jo," she said coming back to them. "I got distracted. This is a lot of beauty to take in. It's mesmerizing," she said, complimenting the house.

"Thank you."

"As you were saying … this is where it gets complicated?" he said smiling at Maitland and then back at Jo.

"Yes, this is definitely where it gets complicated…"

Chapter Thirty-Five
It's Complicated

"Yes, this is where the story gets more complicated. Let's take a U-turn around the staircase. You can see some rooms off to the left and straight ahead covering the back wall there's a very large wall cabinet here and is rounded as it turns to the right to meet the back railing of the staircase. So many would think, this was just built as storage for the maids back in the day. But if you look more closely at the one directly to the left of the staircase landing, you see it has a more modest closet and the shoot for the laundry that goes into the basement, which by the way, is horrifying by itself. That's a whole other story for some other time. Long story short, I access only the washer and dryer down there and some storage directly surrounds that area. It goes deep under the house where light just gets absorbed and it's fucking terrifying. Excuse my French." Jo said and smiled. "I just pretend right now that it doesn't exist because it scares me. God knows what's down there."

They seemed entertained by her storytelling as she continued.

"So, if you look at the maids' cabinet on the left, and then you look at the back wall cabinet, what do you see?" She asked them. They came toward the back wall and looked at it, opened the cabinets and then looked back at the other.

"Oh, yah, I see it," Maitland said.

"Yah, I can see the difference. This one is way more decorative than the other," Weathers said, touching the back wall cabinet.

"Right, one was built for maids to use, The other was made at a different time, much nicer and ornate, but also to cover some things and to create a distraction.

"I have to say," Weathers commented, "that as I'm up here, standing here, I have completely lost my sense of direction and where I am in the house. I mean, I know I haven't seen a tour of the lower level yet but I've seen the front and entered through the back, but this is a weird deprivation feeling right here. I'm visually overwhelmed by all I'm seeing, the rooms behind the staircase, the large wall cabinet and when turning around to see this long hallway with so much to look at, while not being able to orient myself with back windows, my eyes are just pulled to go in the opposite direction of the light at the far end of the hallway. I'm being pulled that way."

"Yes, you get it. It was done on purpose to draw you away from this area. Behind this huge wall cabinet are windows that are so densely hidden in layers of trees and

232

brush that you didn't even notice the shape of the house in this area, right?"

"Yah, I didn't even think to look twice at the landscaping. There was so much it kept my eyes down more to look at it as I walked up. It looked beautiful and dense as you said, and you're right, there was no giveaway on the shape of the house outside, just a lot of landscaping. Evergreens, right? Those are year-round?" Weathers asked.

"Yes. So, we have a lot of year-round trees, evergreens and bushes with berries, ferns that will grow as large as a house if you let them. I'm exaggerating." She smiled. "Some that grow bushy, some that grow up. There are so many evergreen trees that grow very full and there are cypress trees and hedgerow. A lot of thought and planning went into this cover up. You will see that this style closet was used in the rooms and therefore would not necessarily catch attention by anyone as odd since they are used in the bedrooms, even though it's clearly too fancy for a maids closet like the other." She pointed to the maids closet.

"With the windows covered and no way to see out from this space other than the far hall down the hallway facing the front of the house, It's very confusing. There's a slight alcove to these rooms behind the staircase here that prevents you from seeing the windows inside them directly from just standing here. The rooms feel more private with this little alcove architecture. Please, go in and take a look at the rooms." She stood back and let them see the beauty of them. She heard the normal sounds of people admiring a beauty they didn't see every day. It made her smile. She kept being drawn to the end of the hall. The Cold Room was pulling her, but she had to take her time to fill them in on things as they went.

When they came out from viewing the rooms their eyebrows were raised, "Wow, do all the rooms have fireplaces?" Weathers asked.

"Yes," she answered and smiled.

"So cool," Maitland responded.

As they all stood in the alcove, Jo pointed to the far wall across from them, behind the staircase and at the cabinetry that curved on to the far wall.

"That's where the hidden room door used to be." The cabinet curved and was not squared as to give any sense of a square cut of a corner wall or rectangular door, or anything that resembled a natural feature of where a door would have been. It was all smoke and mirrors very well thought out.

They stood quietly looking and making a mental note. They were clearly fascinated by it. They both walked

234

over to touch and open the cabinets to look. They both looked up to the ceiling where the cabinet ended.

"I would have no idea. Even looking at it now and you telling me it's there. I still can't see it. That's amazing." Weathers said.

"Yah, it's pretty incredible," Jo said. "Shall we continue?" she said as a good host.

"The rooms are all much the same in beauty as you will see. Let's just make our way down the hall," and she continued to stop at each room to allow them to look inside each and see them.

"Oh, I see what you mean with the cabinets in the rooms too," Maitland said. "No one would say anything about the one in the hall because they are the same decoratively as in the rooms."

"Right," Jo said. They reached Jo's old room and stepped inside. They both went immediately to the bay widow alcoves and looked out the windows to see the front of the house.

"You know as we came away from that back area and seeing the widows in each room, I began to feel more oriented. It's amazing how that area back there just feels like dead energy to me," Maitland said.

"You're a sensitive, aren't you?" Jo asked her.

"Yah, she sure is," Weathers answered for her and smiled. "She's quite talented at seeing beyond the veil." They both took in the outside view and then turned to Jo. She shut her bedroom door and faced them. They looked at her and their smiles faded slightly.

"I'm sorry. I always feel safer in this room, so I closed the door. I just felt like there are eyes on me while I am talking to you," and she raised her arm to show the hair on end.

"Goose bumps? Me too," and Maitland raised her arm and walked toward Jo to show her.

"Yah. You feel it. So for some reason, this room is like a safe room. I thought it good for you to know. I would recommend you sleep in this room or any of the others but not in the Cold Room. I just feel it's too dangerous to sleep there."

"Are you renting the Cold Room out for the BnB?" Weathers asked.

"No!," Jo replied, dramatically. "It will be part of the daily tours and when a special guest like you comes I will leave it open to them, but not for guests. No one has stayed in there since I've been here, and we only go into the room in twos. I sometimes break the rules though and then pay for it later with nightmares. My mom had a terrible experience in here, trying to reason with the ghost to leave me alone. I found her in here catatonic, and levitating. I know that's hard to believe! And a strange wind from nowhere whipping everything around."

They said nothing, they just listened.

"I have no idea what you'll experience, if anything at all, but regardless, there is the story of the house and at minimum you'll see where the tragedy occurred. I do simply just ask for you to please be careful and work together. Don't be away from each other for too long in this house if you separate. I saw in your videos you both have walkies?"

They both answered yes.

"Please keep them on when separated. When things get too much, if they do, come into this room and shut the door or go downstairs into the kitchen to catch your breath. I have done that often and I just wanted to share that with you, so you know what seems to work. *And*," Jo said cheerfully, trying to change the mood, "if nothing at all happens, you have spent the night in a beautiful Victorian with a very creepy history!"

They both smiled.

"I'm personally hoping that for you. Maitland," Jo said reaching for her hand gently, "as a sensitive, please bubble up your energy, protect it, call in your higher power or source energy and light, whatever your thing is. If you

237

didn't do it already, please do it now. Both of you actually, hell, all of us, let's just take a moment to breathe deep and put an energy bubble around ourselves. So nothing gets in but what you let in."

Maitland reached for Weathers' hand, and they stood there facing one another taking a few deep breaths with closed eyes protecting their energy. When they were done, they faced the door.

Jo walked over to the door and opened it. They came behind her and all stared at the door across the hall.

"That's it, huh?" Weathers asked.

"Yep!"

They stood there for a moment in the doorway of Jo's old room, just looking at it before they crossed the threshold of the safe room.

"Ready?" Jo asked as all their eyes were locked on the Cold Room door.

"Yep, let's do this," Weather said. Maitland concurred with a nod.

Jo took a deep breath and gripped the doorknob and turned.

Chapter Thirty-Six
The Cold Room

The doorknob creaked as she twisted it and opened the door slowly. This was just an ordinary room in a Victorian house, but it had the air of menace you didn't want to awaken by opening the doors fast. Opening slowly allowed a sort of mental preparation for what you might see or feel. Although no peril ever came to her just by opening the door, still, it was a precaution she took each and every time. Perhaps, in a weird way, a sort of announcement to what was there, and that she was coming in.

She pushed the door fully open and with Maitland and Weathers standing behind her, she stood in front of the door looking at the room but not yet moving forward. She allowed them a moment to take it in and she allowed herself a moment to 'feel' the room. She was certain Maitland was experiencing the same thing. It had a dreary sort of feeling for no perceivable reason.

"It's lovely, but I hate it." Maitland said. "No offense," she said turning to Jo and then peeling her eyes back to the room.

"None taken," Jo said still looking into the room and around as if looking for something. One small, demented child perhaps.

239

"Fantastic," Weathers said and looked down at Jo. "May we?"

"Oh, yes, certainly." Jo said, and hers were the first feet to cross the threshold. They all stepped into the room.

"Please, look around."

Jo stood by the door so she could keep her eyes on the landscape view of the room and the two of them who went in different directions. Maitland toward the window to the front of the house, looking at the furnishings, wallpaper and decorations perfectly placed on end tables and the desk. Weathers in the direction to the left to the bathroom, leaving only one area left to explore.

"You have done a wonderful job with this room," Weathers said.

"Yes," Maitland said. "It's really beautiful. But it feels … hmm … ugly, shall I say, in here? I get the distinct feeling of not being wanted in this room." Maitland froze for a moment. Something was happening.

Jo looked at Weathers. He put out his hand to pause all talking while watching Maitland's face and letting her have her moment.

She looked up at Weathers. "I just heard 'Get Out'," she whispered.

Weathers looked back at Jo, "Maitland, as I said earlier, sees and hears beyond the veil. She is clairvoyant and clairaudient. You heard this internally, Mait, or in the environment?"

"Internal sound," she said.

"The room has a certain charge, doesn't it?" he asked.

"Indeed. This room from the first day had a heaviness to it. I felt it even from outside when I pulled in. My eyes were drawn to this front room from the very first."

Maitland and Weathers both looked at each other. "We felt the same thing when we drove up. Of course, we had no idea where the Cold Room was in the house, but we both stopped to look at the house when we drove in, and both of us commented that we kept having our eyes drawn to this window. Isn't that interesting?"

"Yah, definitely. It seems to be what most people do upon walking up to this house. I don't think people realize initially why they do it, but they 'feel' *something,* and their eyes automatically just go up to this room. I see the mail man do it all the time. I think he gets the creeps walking up to the house. He seems to have a little more speed coming and going than he does with the other houses," she said with a smirk on her face.

They all laughed and then turned back to face the closet that was on the opposite wall from the bathroom, directly across the room from it.

"So, that's the entrance then?" Weathers asked. "To the real Cold Room?" referring to her comment before about the room they were standing really being the Cold Room suite, and that the real Cold Room lay behind the wall, although they all just called both the Cold Room. They could never be separated now. They were as one unit, although what lay behind the wall was much more scary.

"Yah. Ready?"

They both agreed and she opened the door and secured it open with the hook. She had learned from her initial experience of the door slamming shut on her and Layce that she would not allow that to happen again. They noticed and made a mental note. A precaution was put in place including an electric hurricane lamp permanently hung on a hook in the closet should the closet light go out as it did before when she and Layce discovered the hidden room. The door had slammed shut locking them in and the light had flickered out. That mistake would not happen again.

She opened the beautifully made closet placed in what had been a sort of corner, positioned in a way that

242

one could not know the true depth from the outside due to the many curves and cuts of the architecture in that area of the room. The architect played with smoke and mirrors much like the Winchester Mystery House, with doors opening to steep falls, windows in the ceiling of the kitchen so the mistress could see down and watch the staff (that backfired because of light glare), or staircases that led to ceilings. There was mischief in the architecture in the Purdy House as well. It was incredible and created a feeling that you just didn't know what you would see once you opened the door. Just like in the hallway behind the staircase, this floor to ceiling closet had rounded edges and the other shapes and curvatures left one curious and created a slight feeling of discombobulation. A closet yes, but surely not expecting the depth of the closet in this room. The depth alone seemed off.

"Oh, wow," Weathers said as he poked his head in. "It's much deeper than I expected. Is there a light?" he asked Jo.

She stepped inside the center, slightly disappearing into the darkness and pulled the string to turn the light on. It flickered. Immediately they saw the electric hurricane light she had put in there hanging on a hook. She had made sure to install something that required no flame for safety reasons and could serve as their backup light. She turned it on.

They immediately looked to the large hole in the wall to the right, and then down at the open compartment in the floor where they had found hair and teeth tucked away in a little box hidden under a plank of wood in the corner, more than usual for a memento. It was confiscated by the police on that fateful day of discovery, and she was glad to have it out of the house.

"We found the plank of wood that was discolored in the corner," she pointed in the direction, "when we were cleaning out the closet. The previous owners left a box as well, so we had the realtor ship that back to the owners. I didn't even care to look inside it. It was clearly a recently packed box, so we just got rid of it. Go ahead, look what's back there, well, its empty now, but the feeling is still palpable, at least to me," she said.

"Oh, I agree," Maitland said.

"I just want to warn you both, please, before we go back there, okay? Just, bubble up again, please. I think, clairvoyance or not, we're human with senses and knowing what happened in the room back there is beyond what we can imagine horrible to be. And that energy has a weight to it that isn't pleasant to be around. We won't stay in there long; I only stay a minute or two. You of course can do what you want when you're on your own, but when we go as a group, we will exit about a minute later. I do this for me. I just don't like being in there and I won't feel good leaving you there, okay? What you do on your own time is up to you, later. This is just a quick tour. Sound good?"

They agreed and all crouched and climbed through the hole in the wall and immediately were dropped into a different world frozen in time. Dust and spiders, cobwebs, a musty smell, and a darkness save for the hurricane lamp Jo was now holding to lead them the way down a short hall. The wallpaper was peeling from the walls, completely different in style from the house now, clearly original. At the end of the hall was a slight light that managed to break through the dense brush outside that had concealed the room.

As she walked slowly down the hall with them following, she said, "I had pulled the covering off one of the windows when we found the room, and recently pulled the other window covering down to see outside, well, what I could see. Nothing really but dense brush, the same as the other window. There's no way to orient yourself at all. But it does manage to let in some light into the room now as you can see. You will see on the far left in the room the door that is now covered in the back hallway behind the staircase with that cabinet. It will all make sense when you see it." She continued to walk them down the hallway passing an old bathroom never used again once sealed. "Oh also, please don't touch the walls or anything in here. I have not cleaned, nor will I, and I don't want you to get hurt or cut in any way on anything peeling or sharp."

Maitland and Weathers were like most people who began to enter that horrible place, stunned into silence to prepare mentally and emotionally to see the room of legend and horror. Most people couldn't imagine such atrocities, so emotions tended to rise in the moment. The reality sank in. Before being there, it was just a story.

They stepped into the open room and Jo allowed them to look and take it in. The room was made up of the same things all the others had, , a fireplace, odd shapes and corners in the architecture, a closet, but it held none of the warmth. The room began to creak as they walked on the floorboards, , and Jo explained some of what they had found.

"We found about a dozen or so children here, murdered and ripped apart like they were dolls. She did what she pleased with them once she got them in here. We believe she killed them right away and then ..." her voice faded. "Children ranging in age from three months old to two, some with lips sewn shut with large spindle

Sufani Weisman-Garza

thread and eyelids sewn open – some of the skin was intact still, as though the children preserved some of their bodies, seemingly waiting for someone to someday know what she had done to them." Jo swallowed hard. It was hard to believe, even still, that this was in her house and still choked her up to recount the tale.

Maitland and Weathers' faces changed. They were no longer Grimm Night Detective but two people who had just heard the worst story of their lives and she saw tears develop in Weathers' eyes. It got to him.

"That is … I can't even imagine … there are no words." His voice cracked.

Maitland sniffled. The story was too sad for anyone to take in without reaction.

"We found them hanging on the walls like dolls," and Jo motioned to the areas on the walls where they had been. "There was a table in the room here where she 'played' and there were blood splatters and dental tools. Of course, all of that has been taken into custody as evidence. "

"Dental tools?" Maitland asked.

"Yes. Her father was a dentist."

"Oh!" Her face looked down thinking of the horror of it. "Did she …?

247

"Yes, she removed all their teeth, well, those old enough to have them. I have said to Layce before, we can only hope she did that after they were …" she cleared her throat with emotion catching up to her, "gone." She had thought about that before and deduced it would have had to be done that way or the parents would have surely heard the terrible screams of children. No one could 'not' hear a baby's cry. She didn't have the heart to say that now, although it was part of the tour script that she would share with them later for their knowledge and research of the house.

There was a hush as they took in the story and turned individually to take in the room and look at it all. Maitland walked over to the door that was covered, and Weathers followed. A natural reaction to get one's mind off the horrific story. A chill entered the room and Maitland instantly grabbed both her arms and shivered. The wall began to make creaking, settling noises that are normal for a house to make from time to time, but not like this. They both turned around to face Jo. Jo got that feeling that always came over her when something was present that was not of this world. An internal rush of heat from head to toe in a few seconds. Her body reacted with adrenaline.

"It's time to go."

248

As she said this, Weathers grabbed Maitland's hand to hold as they were leaving. He stepped forward and a gust of dust blew violently in his face. He startled and choked, jolting to a dead stop with surprise, doubled over and coughing fiercely. Maitland yelped and felt the room change. It seemed even darker in the room than it had been just seconds ago and much colder, and the candle flicker of the lamp became more apparent.

"Are you okay?" Maitland said, leaning under her husband who was bent over coughing, trying to get the dust out of his nose and lungs. Her face scrunched in concern.

"Out, now!" Jo grabbed both their arms ushering them into the hallway pushing them toward the hole in the wall while Weathers continued to cough violently.

"Maitland, get him out through the hole first and keep going. Get out of this room. I will be right behind you."

Maitland did as she was told. Weathers' brutal coughing did not settle. Jo followed directly behind them, gently moving Maitland forward. It was natural to freeze in an emergency and want to tend to her husband, but that would need to happen in the hallway and out of that room.

The closet remained open, thanks to the hook she installed. They exited the closet, Jo turned off the hurricane lamp and quickly hung it back up, then pulled the string of the closet light, exited, and closed the door to the closet as Maitland and Weathers left the room. Layce, Ginni and Hank were standing at the top of the staircase having heard the commotion and were watching as Weathers continued to cough violently.

Jo opened the Safe Room door and pushed them in.

"Sit on the bed," Jo directed, as she went into the bathroom and used one of the guest drinking cups to fill with water for him. She ripped off the plastic covering, and threw the wrapper hastily, filled it with water and handed it to Maitland and then went to the hallway and told the girls it was okay, and to go wait in the kitchen. They'd be down in a minute. They all understood and went back down. Their faces all showed worry, but none wanted to go near the Cold Room and didn't try.

Weathers' coughing began to subside and he took intermittent drinks of water between the coughing. He began to say something as the coughing became less violent. In between coughs, hack, hack, hack, "Fucking," hack, hack, hack, "Awesome," and right then and there was relief. His sense of humor and intrigue was still attached. His cough began to settle until there was none. He finished the water and took a moment to steady himself after this attack.

"Welcome to the Cold Room," Jo said sarcastically.

"*Wow*," Maitland said. "That was *really* intense. Babe, are you okay?"

"Yah, I'm good now."

"Are you ready to walk?" Jo asked Weathers.

He stood up strong, Maitland touched his arm and held on to him, more for herself as he had fully recovered. He was like her and didn't scare easily.

"Yah! How about that coffee?" he asked.

Jo smiled and opened the door exiting first and blocking the Cold Room door and motioned for them to go out and down the hall. Lacye had come back up and was standing at the top of the stairs and Jo motioned to her with her eyes a protective pass off. She felt protective and would not allow anything further in this moment to happen to them. However, she knew full well she couldn't protect them from their stay tonight, in the Cold Room, and the shadows that lurked around every corner of the Purdy House.

They now had a taste of what could happen, and they would have to choose for themselves whether to take that risk, or not!

Chapter Thirty-Seven
Kitchen Talk

"Oh yah, we're down," Weathers said with excitement when Jo asked whether or not they wanted to continue. "We're so down for this. I can't believe that just happened."

"Holy Moly, that was scary," Hank said after hearing a condensed summary from Jo on what had transpired, as they all stood in the kitchen drinking coffee and Jo, Weathers and Maitland got their bearings again.

"Hank, are you still okay with working here? This is your first," she paused a moment to choose her words, "*experience*, with the Cold Room." Jo knew it was one thing to think about spooky fun and then to live it.

"Oh, for sure. Plus, I'm gonna be in the gift shop anyway."

"That may be worse," Ginni said playfully under her breath towards Layce's ear, and Layce elbowed her in the arm. They both laughed. Hank looked at them inquisitively.

"We'll fill you in later," Ginni said and took another sip of coffee.

Hank just smiled and said, "Ok."

"So, Maitland and Weathers, please put my cell number in your phone right now. In case you need me at any time while you're in here today and overnight, text or call me. And I mean, anytime. Listen to your instincts and if anything happens, I'm right outside to help out at any moment to come in." The two had only her professional land line in the cottage house and email prior and now they would be more personally connected.

They exchanged cell numbers, and all finished their coffee. Ginni took ownership of the lot and was tidying up the kitchen. This was to be her work area now in the Purdy House, so it seemed fitting. Everyone thanked Ginni as she took their cups, rinsed them and put them in the dishwasher.

"So, question," Jo said to the Grimm Night Detectives, "What exactly do you guys do in here? Is there a bunch of equipment you bring in, you know, ghost hunting gear? I don't recall seeing a lot of that on your channel, but, you know, I haven't seen too much of your work. Just enough to get a sense of what you do."

"No, we don't do the whole 'Ghost Adventures' setup up. We aren't ghost hunters per se, but deal with all things odd and macabre. We will have a few things in here for fun and will record with some tools that have really worked for us. But Maitland is the best tool we got," and he smiled over at his gal and touched her hand. "By the way, it is a crazy different feeling down here. I feel totally relaxed down here and it's almost like what just happened up there is a distant memory or something. Almost like a dream, like it didn't happen, but I know it did."

"Yep, that is exactly what it's like living here. I think that's how people were able to live here. You get accustomed to it in a way. the weird becomes the new normal and it feels so unrealistic after you've had the experience that maybe your brain just settles on thinking of it as a story, not so much a reality. But it is. It's a really strange feeling."

Ginni and Layce were agreeing with her, having been with Jo and the house almost from the beginning.

There was a knock on the front door.

"Hello," a deep voice called out from the front of the house. Jo leaned left to see passed the dining room and living room to try to see the front door and saw that it was Donovan.

"DeeDee," Layce called out happily and ran to the front door to let him in.

"This is our friend Donovan," Jo said. "He's a therapist but more importantly a friend. He has supported me through my settling in here, as a friend," she said with emphasis on friend. "He's been with me through the initial craziness of things happening in this house and I needed his rational mind to double check me and what was happening. He really provided a lot of support and indeed found this house is…"

"Everyone, DeeDee," Layce said as they entered the kitchen, introducing him to everyone who had not yet met him.

"Whoa, there's a lot of people in here," he said, surprised, and smiled. "Hi, I'm Donovan," he said to Grimm Night and shook their hands. Layce had already filled him in on who they were and the basics on her way back to the kitchen. The girl talked fast.

"Hey Hank, What's up?" he said rhetorically looking at her and carried on. She responded with a friendly hey back. "I Just wanted to wish you luck with the opening," he said to Jo.

Jo smiled a warm smile at him. She thought his kindness had no bounds and she was always surprised by it. He was truly a friend to her and expressed it so well.

"Here," he said walking over to her and taking one of her hands and dropping something in her palm. "My Mom wanted me to give this to you as a blessing."

Jo looked in her palm and it was a small coin decoratively wrapped in gold with turquoise beads around it.

"Oh, this is lovely," she said, "I couldn't take this, it must be a family heirloom." And she held up the charm hanging from a gold necklace admiring it as the others also looked at it. There was an approving coo from the women looking at it.

"She wanted you to have it. Besides, it's not real gold, or a family heirloom. It's a tapahueso, something Panamanians wear in their traditional folklore festivities. There's a whole outfit that goes with it too, but I thought it might be a bit much," he said playfully. "Also, it's stainless steel so it won't turn your neck green. My Mom said you could just keep it in your pocket for good luck, blessings or protection, whatever you need. You don't have to wear it." He seemed to get a little embarrassed that he had an audience for this conversation and moved on. "Anyway, I have to get back to the office for an appointment," and he pointed his thumb to the door."

"Thank you so much, Donovan," Jo said, touched. "Please thank your mom for me," and she gave him a hug. The group looked on, smiling and quiet.

"I will. I'll show myself out. Sorry to interrupt everyone," he said, turning to leave.

"Say, Donovan," Weathers called out. "I was briefed that you were of great support and sort of played devil's advocate to Jo's paranormal happenings around here. "

256

Donovan looked at Jo and smiled, "I suppose you could say that. I think Jo wanted a second opinion from a science thinking person."

"When we're done here, may we also interview you, briefly?"

He looked at Jo for approval. It was up to her. Of course, he would share nothing personal about their therapy which was now shorter than their budding friendship in duration.

She looked at him approvingly, fully trusting him.

"Donovan you have my permission to share anything you like with them and what's been going on in this house from your point of view."

He acknowledged her approval. "Ok, here's my card. Give me a text when you'd like to meet and I'd be happy to help," and with that he took his leave and went back to his office.

Jo put the pendant in her pocket, knowing she could use all the luck and protection she could get.

Layce stood from her chair and stretched. Hank also stood and went to use the restroom.

"Jo, to answer your question about what we'll do, we do use a few tools but we're not a ghost hunting operation per se, but we do do ghost hunting. We don't really call it that though. We're more focused on the things

257

in life in general that are odd or can't be explained. We aren't so much interested in a bunch of equipment readings but what we experience. We also don't care too much about proving anything but, rather, sharing a story. There will always be people who don't believe, and people who do. We aren't interested in convincing people to believe but in sharing an intriguing story. We want people to listen more than anything and then feel a sense of connection if they are going through something similar. So far, that approach has worked." He smiled at her, and Maitland looked at her intently.

"I like that," Jo said.

"So just like what happened right now. All we have is our stories to share. It wasn't filmed. But our community trusts us and knows that what we say, we really experience. Of course, we'll go back and film and perhaps catch more. We will use a K2 meter with just measuring electromagnetic fields that some say raise when a ghost is present. We'll do a baseline around the house on camera first because a home's electrical can also affect the meter. We also use a Frank's box or ghost box. Frank's Box is designed specifically to capture EVP, electrical voice phenomena. It's basically a broken radio that sweeps through channels creating a white noise and sometimes a voice clearly comes through. It's great for affect in videos

258

and pretty creepy when the conversation is intelligent. Like, answering specifically the questions you are asking."

Hank entered back into the room and leaned against the counter listening.

"That's interesting. I have seen some of this stuff on tv but didn't really know the name of the equipment. That's really cool," Jo said.

"So," Weathers said, "the plan is to get started checking things out. We'll be filming the house and the property as we do our walk-throughs. So, if there is anything you want off limits, please let us know now so we can be aware of it. Once the video is out, we won't make any changes or edits to it. If there is anything off limits, we'll put it in writing and we'll all sign it so there's no confusion or anyone upset later that something they didn't want released to the public is out there. Is there anything?" he asked.

Jo paused for a moment thinking and looked at Layce as well. "The only thing you won't have access to is our cottage house. You won't have keys to it anyway and I don't mind you filming the outside, which will be hard to miss when you're filming the grounds anyway."

Maitland pulled out her phone and was typing away and then Jo and Weathers got pinged; they both got a text and checked it.

"Hello, it's me, Maitland. Just confirming that we have permission to film everything on the grounds inside and out, except the inside of the cottage house, but the outside of the cottage house is fine to film. All in favor say aye."

Weather and Jo both texted.

Jo's text: "Aye."

Weathers text: "Aye."

Maitland's reply: "Aye and agreed upon. Yay!"

Jo looked up from her phone to the girls who had no idea what was said.

"We just all agreed."

"Excellent," Layce said, while Ginni and Hank just smiled at Jo.

"Ok, well, I have to walk the dogs and give them their afternoon treat," Jo said. She stepped up to Weathers and pulled two keys out of her pocket. "Here 's the skeleton key to the front of the house," she handed it over, "and here is the modern key to the backdoor." She turned to face Maitland, not wanting to leave her out and handed it to her.

"Cool," Maitland said and looked down and smiled. She was clearly excited to be getting started.

"I'll be in the cottage house when you need me, and if I go anywhere, it will be quick errands. You can text

260

me if I'm not here, or even if I am, if you need me. Oh, but remember," she said.

The Grimm Night Detectives looked at her intently.

"Do not go into the yurt without telling me, okay? If I'm out and about, still please text me what time you enter and when you set the annunciator time too, so I know. Other than that, it's all yours."

They agreed.

With that the group began to break up and they all walked toward the back door, stepping through it one by one.

Jo closed the door, left it unlocked, and the screen slammed shut as they all walked down the stairs.

Maitland and Weathers clearly had things to retrieve from their SUV, including their bags. Their set up would take time.

Jo worried but didn't dare ask what room they would sleep in tonight. They had already emailed in their signed waiver, so it was up to them now.

The house inside was silent.

Save for the sound of the echoing voice of a distant child's devious and gleeful laughter bouncing from room to room, whipping up a wind that could only be from the open gates of hell.

Sufani Weisman-Garza

Chapter Thirty-Eight
Alone At Last

Maitland and Weathers began taking things out of their opened SUV hatch and lifting light stands and filming tripods out of the back. There was a lot of filming equipment that would be set up around the house to capture anything. Their channel mostly focused on a hand-held camera, and they would take people on a tour with this as they talked about what they were seeing and feeling, and always considered the stories of the owners of said business or home. They would always research local lore if there was any and would almost always talk with neighbors or townspeople about what they knew about a given place to make a fully rounded picture for the viewers. At the same time, it felt very casual and effortless. It was a ritual they had developed over the years, and it was a well-oiled machine now.

After about fifteen minutes of maneuvering equipment and discussing where things would go, they shut the hatch door and carried the first batch of equipment and lighting toward the house. Maitland looked over to the cottage window to see Jo smiling at her and waiving with her "Eek," face. Maitland smiled and laughed.

"Look at Jo in the window."

Weathers looked over and smiled at Jo. "She's pretty cool, huh?"

"I really like her. It's too bad this is happening to her, but I guess it's meant to be. She's really taking it in stride and building it into her life. Kudos to her."

"Yah, a lot of people would cut and run," Weathers said as they began to climb the stairs up to the back door.

"I sense a deep sadness in her, but a toughness too. Do we know anything about her background yet?"

"No, I didn't ask yet. We'll get that story before we finish up if she's open to it."

They took the stairs up, reached the top of the stairs at the back door and twisted the knob to go in. It wouldn't twist.

Maitland put down her equipment and brought out her phone. This was where it would start. She pressed record.

Weathers began, facing the camera and talking while stretching his fingers out expressively like little knives. "We're at the infamous Purdy House and just got the introductory tour that was incredible. More about what happened soon. But right now, as we began to bring equipment into the house, the unlocked door we just walked out of, is now not allowing us in. We've been told that this same thing happened to the owner the day she

263

moved in." He turned away from the camera again and Maitland moved to the side so the frame was not blocked as he tried the knob again on camera. Still, it would not turn.

"Let's have the key, Mait," and Maitland handed him the modern key to open the back door. He put it in the lock and turned to the camera. "Let's see," and he turned the key and they heard the click of a lock turning. "Yes," he said, "Now the thing that is freaky is that we just left this house and the door was not locked when we exited , there is no one in the house, we watched everyone leave with us, and somehow the door was then locked," and as he said that and expected the door knob to turn and let him in, he leaned his weight into the door and it did not budge.

"What the hell!" he said, confused. Maitland was still filming the real reactions of Weathers. "Let me try again."

He did so and the same click, the same turn of the knob, the same door would not budge as though something was playing a game of him turning the lock open and someone inside turning it back shut.

"Wow, we aren't even in the house yet, and you can see already why this house is infamous. Okay, Plan B," he said to the camera. "We have a skeleton key that is the original house key that was never changed out. I love that. We'll go around the front and see if the house lets us in."

264

They set down whatever equipment they retained in their hands other than the filming camera Maitland was using. They walked back down the stairs and around towards the front of the house. The camera was glued to Weathers.

The grounds were empty of anyone, and Maitland filmed him walking down the stairs, and all the way to the front of the house while capturing landscaping, the grey sky and some of the grounds that would look great in the shot. When they got to the front of the house, Maitland remained further away from the house to capture his full body and the house in front of the stairs as he faced the house and she slowly walked toward him. Her camera was on a gimbal that made the walk smooth and camera steady. Once she was a foot away from him, he instinctively felt her and began his ascent up the front steps. Their approach was cinematic. She followed behind enough to capture his whole body and movements. When back at the front door the shot zoomed in on the screen opening, the skeleton key being pulled out of his pocket and placed in the lock and he turned it, heard the click and turned the knob. He pushed on it and to his surprise, the door swung open. The house made a noise like a suction or like the house exhaling breath.

Maitland kept the camera rolling, "Wait, wasn't the front door open too when Donovan left?"

Weathers' eyebrows went up and he smiled. He had forgotten that in all the commotion. "Quickly, follow me," he said to the camera and went straight down the hallway on the left, passing the living room on the right, library on the left, passing the front staircase and the hallway's huge wall bookshelf, straight back to the backdoor that just refused them entrance. When he got to the back door he instructed Maitland, "Zoom in on the door hardware." He walked up to it and stood aside not touching it. The door was not locked. Once Mait captured it on camera she held it there for his large hand to grip the knob and turn it. He pulled and the door opened. He turned back to the camera dumbfounded and with a joyful smirk.

"Already, it begins," he said. "So much more to come." With that he made a downward motion with his hand that was their signal to stop filming. She did.

"This is gonna be interesting," Maitland said. Weathers just nodded and opened the screen. Maitland put her phone in her pocket, and they began the work of getting everything they left on the back steps into the house and continued outside to get what remained of their things, including their bags for the night.

They left the door open in front and back for the time being even though the weather outside had turned colder and the sky a darker grey. It looked as though rain was on the way, which would only enhance the filming. Rain, while filming in a haunted house. What could be more perfect?

"Hopefully, the screens will cooperate," Maitland said as they approached the SUV to gather their things.

"It's not the screens I'm worried about." Weathers said as he opened the SUV hatch. "It's whatever it was that had the power to manipulate hardware at will, or blow dust in my face out of nowhere, that does," and with that the last of their items were in hand as they walked up the stairs, and into the house through the back door.

The door closed tightly behind them. The clouds grew even darker. Lighting struck. It started to rain.

Chapter Thirty-Nine
It Begins

Maitland and Weathers spent a good few hours setting up lighting and stationary cameras in the rooms in the house they planned to take their audience through, the hallways, the living spaces, some of the rooms upstairs especially the safe room, staircases, the Cold Room suite and the Cold Room itself. They worked together in the Cold Room and did not sperate as Jo had instructed them. Cameras were placed in the Cold Room suite, the closet, the hallway through the hole to the Cold Room, and the Cold Room itself. During setup nothing occurred but business as usual, although both felt the electricity in the air and had the feeling of being on edge, as though waiting for something to happen.

"So, I was thinking we'll start in the living room, just below where the Cold Room is and where the pouring of the teeth happened and go from there. What do you think?" Weathers asked Maitland.

"That's perfect," she agreed adjusting the lighting on him.

Before they began filming, they meticulously plotted out the tour path of the house to make sure that where they went the lights were perfectly placed as well as not in

268

the shot. And of course, they would adjust along the way. Her camera was on the gimbal, which allowed walking with the camera easy, and for amazing shots while moving from different angles. She was ready to go.

"Ready," she asked.

"Yes," he answered.

RECORD

"We're standing in one of the most haunted houses in Washington State," he said with his fingers expressive and daggerlike, Gothic rings and finger tattoos clearly displayed. "This house," he looked around, "this beautiful house, was built in the 1890s." He stopped to look around. "But as beautiful as this is, it's also rumored to be haunted, and has the most horrific history, one of the worst I've heard. But before we get to that, I want to show you a little of this house and the grounds so you can see just how beautiful it is. We can hardly believe we're standing in it, and better yet, we're gonna stay in it, overnight! So, with that, let's get started."

RECORDING STOPPED

269

"That was perfect," Maitland said looking directly at him and not through the camera.

Weathers positioned himself and took a deep breath, "Ok, I'm ready."

RECORD

"So, let's start right here," he said looking around and up. "Now, this house is the scene of not just one grisly murder, that took place just above me," and he pointed to the room above. The camera slightly panned up. "But it was the home of many grisly murders. What makes this story so horrific is that the murders were of children, and the murderer?" He paused for effect, "was a child herself." He walked around the living room admiring it as the camera followed, so the viewer could see the historic beauty, architecture and décor as he talked.

"Now the original owner of this house was a dentist, Mr. Purdy." He walked toward the library room, and then into the library and the camera followed behind him as he went to the large bookcase on the wall and took a large volume out, filming slightly off to his side to catch his profile so as to not always be filming the back of his head, and he

270

periodically looked at the camera as he moved, talked and looked around at the home.

"He had a wife and child that lived here. I would imagine they seemed like a normal, if not *elite* family. There were servants who cooked and cleaned," he said as he exited the library out into the hall and began walking past the front staircase and touching the beautiful ornate woodwork of the banister, passing the bookshelves in the hallway past the front staircase letting his fingers pass over the books that lined the hallway and walked toward the back staircase, "a maids' cottage out back, a maids' station upstairs," he pointed up as the camera now faced him, getting the back staircase banister, his torso and his face. Standing directly in front of the staircase periodically looking up with one foot on the first step, he went on, "but this house has something no other home in the area has," he said, looking up the staircase with a trepidation he really felt, "a room of a serial killer." His mind flashed to being in the Cold Room and how it felt, the compassion for the children and terror of that room, and it showed on his face, "what they now call, the Cold Room. A hidden room that was revealed to the current owner only recently, and upon her terrifying

271

discovery, the ghost of the Cold Room, in an unbelievable paranormal event, rained down teeth in impossible numbers, in the room we began this video in, "and he walked through the kitchen, dining room and back into the living room as the camera followed him, "in a shower of ivory rage, as though the child serial killer was in a fury for having been discovered." He paused.

"*What happened here?*" He looked up at the ceiling and got a chill. " What happened here?" he said looking around with his voice getting quieter. "What happened here?" he said, looking directly into the camera. "Well, we many never know for sure. But one thing we do know, it's said that the serial killer … well … she's still in this house. And we're gonna spend the night here. Are we crazy?"

Weathers stepped over to Maitland and took the gimbal hand held from her and asked again turning the camera on her, "Maitland, are we crazy for staying the night here?"

"Yes. Yes, we are?" she answered calmly and with a mild smile.

He handed the camera back to her and she continued filming.

"So, what we want to do," he said more lightly talking directly to his audience, fingers again dagger like and expressive, "is take you on a tour of the house, show you the rooms, show you the grounds, and then just follow us as we ourselves take a deeper look at the house, and enjoy ourselves here. Now, I will tell you, we had a terrifying experience already when we did actually go into the Cold Room when we received our tour of the house. I'll explain that later when we're up there with you. And the owner herself said she couldn't guarantee that we'd have any paranormal activity. I think she is kind of hoping we don't," he said, talking to Maitland directly, but would leave that in the cut. She spoke off camera still watching him.

"Yah, I agree. I saw genuine worry in her eyes for us, actually."

He continued, "But she said that no matter what, we are staying in the infamous home of a serial killer of children, and that by itself would be enough. I gotta tell you, knowing that … it's freaking spine-chilling to stay somewhere knowing that happened where you're gonna lay your head down for the night. The weird thing is, it's juxtaposed with such opulent beauty and warmth in some parts of the

273

house, while others are downright cold, dark and disconcerting."

"Ok, let's talk about what's gonna happen. We set up stationary cameras as well and we'll do a baseline sweep with the K2 of electrical to make sure if there is any electrical changes that happen, we know what the baseline is. We will also play with the Frank's Box when in the Cold Room. I'm kind of scared to do that," he said to Maitland.

"Me too," she said behind the camera. "It's always scary to get a voice that comes back to you from beyond the veil through the voice box, but especially knowing that the voice that could come back truly is evil."

"But" Weathers said. We're gonna do it for you. "So here we go," he stepped forward and looked deep into the camera. "Are we crazy?" he took a deep breath.

RECORDING STOPPED

"That was great."

"Okay, good. So, let's go for a walk around the grounds and I'll film you walking through it as usual. You'll need your hood on, it's raining. I can do voice over and you just talk where you feel inspired. Do you want an umbrella? Well, the rain seems to have stopped, at the moment, I think." They looked out the window in the living room.

"This is a good time to get ground shots," Maitland said. "No umbrella. I don't think Pacific North Westerners use umbrellas, right? Isn't that their thing? No umbrellas?"

"Yah, they're kind of known for not using them. They just wear hoodies, beanies and hats, from what I've seen. Someone told me once when we were in Oregon that you could always tell a tourist by if they use an umbrella." They both laughed. They walked toward the back of the house to go outside and get the front and back ground shots.

"Should we tell Jo we want to go into the yurt?" Maitland asked.

"No, let's focus on the house first, but just make sure initially to get good ground shots before the weather gets too hard to get good ones. We can save the yurt for the end if there's time to get it in. We can actually just shoot some video of the inside at the end, but I don't know if we'll have time to go inside. We'll see," Weathers said.

"Agreed. The most important part is to get the house, the grounds and the Cold Room," Maitland confirmed.

275

So, without a hitch, they went to the back door, Maitland in front, and he began filming her walking in front of him, eight to ten feet in front of him, down the stairs and through the pathways on the grounds. She touched the picket fence of the cottage house and the camera scanned it, and the vast grounds landscaping, the grey sky, some of the trees showing the skeleton of their bones beginning to bud for spring while filming the lush evergreen trees, bushes and ferns that stayed full all year round. They found a little green area tucked away with a bench and even a tree swing in a corner of the garden. The camera focused on that swing. Although almost definitely not original to the house, it was an eerie shot just the same when thinking of what happened to the children in Purdy House, and the scary child who did it. It was hard to fathom innocence this way.

She walked the pathway to the yurt and went onto the porch and peeked into the window, and then away from the porch and back to the grounds again. She walked and stood in front of the fountain, walked through the garden area where plants and trees were both awakening from winter and also annuals that remained lush. She stood facing a portion of the back of the house covered in dense shrubbery and just looking at it. It felt dark, big, old, foreboding. It had such a strong presence even from the outside. It was not welcoming, or friendly feeling. Its structure itself left the impression that one should *be careful.*

She felt a sprinkle on her head and for the camera, pulled up the hood of her black bat jacket, with her neon long yellow hair pouring out over each shoulder. She paused and looked up at the dark grey sky. Weathers checked the time on the phone, and it was after three pm. Sundown was around 6:30 this time of year, he believed. So, it was good that they were getting the shots now. Time was flying. The rain began even harder. Weathers opened the tripod of the gimbal and set it on the fountain edge stationary and allowed the camera to catch them together looking and walking around the area to get a shot of them both there.

They stood in the rain in the garden and found themselves standing behind the deep brush that camouflaged the Cold Room. They stood in the garden looking up and seeing nothing but trees and plants, and at a house so ominous, it was both beauty and beast.

They ended the recording and began to gather the camera and make their way back to the house.

The curtain of the back door window billowed back in place.

Chapter Forty
The Rain Came Down

Jo's cell phone rang in the cottage. She was sitting at her desk with the dogs playing with their toys and she tossed a ball to Nos who wanted to play. Ferrah came to her ankle, sniffed and then sat and leaned on her looking up. She gave her a little head scratch.

"Hey, girl. How you doing?" and she smiled at Ferrah. Such cute dogs.

She picked up on the second ring.

"Hey, Lacye."

Layce asked a question.

"Yah, I've seen them out on the grounds. I think they're about to start their filming inside. By the way, just making sure you feel ready for tomorrow. The big day." There was a pause as she listened to Layce.

"You checked the schedule, too, right?" she paused while listening.

"Yah, me too. I think it was a good move to not start the spa until next week to give you some time to get your bearings. Keep in mind, Sis, that if the touring and doing massage is too much, you can just manage tours. You did line up the other gal and we can ask her to take over the massage aspect when and if you want to. I don't want you too overwhelmed."

"Yah, let's play that by ear," Layce said. "I'm super excited for tomorrow. And right now, for Grimm Night Detective to be there. So cool."

"Is Ginni good and feeling ready?" There was a pause while Layce spoke. "Ok, good. Tell her to call me if she needs anything, otherwise I'll see you both in the am tomorrow to huddle before guests start arriving. Can you check in with Hank please and make sure she's good and see if she needs anything or has any questions?"

"Ok," Layce said.

"Ok, thanks, Sis. Love you."

Layce said she loved her back and they hung up the phone.

Jo walked over to the cottage living room window once more and looked out as the rain came down, and looked at the big house, from the safety of her own room. She felt nervous for the couple in there and wondered if she had done the right thing by letting them in there by themselves. But then she rationalized, the guests will be in there by themselves when they sleep. The only difference is that none would be allowed in the Cold Room, and that was the part that worried her. Her thoughts grew dark,

279

like the day, as she felt a daydream haze come over her, until Tu barked.

She snapped out of it.

"Want a treat," she said when she turned to them in her mousy playful voice and the dogs all looked up at her and danced on the floor in a unanimous, "Yes."

She left the window and forgot about the house that had two souls in it. They were on their own now.

Chapter Forty-One
A Night Alone

The control center screens were set in the dining area. The area itself had been decorated with one large six-seater table, and six more smaller round tables on either side of the large one in the middle to accommodate guests who wanted to come down to eat. Jo had arranged it for a community feeling with long gold tablecloth covers and cloth napkins, antique plateware would be used, mismatched and eclectic, all purchased from the local antique stores. Each piece was handpicked for beauty and artistic merit. They were pieces perhaps left behind from a generation that no longer collected china for fancy gatherings or holidays, perhaps sets were broken, and donated because they no longer had a match. Like her. Each piece told a story and was why she loved antiques, and what had made her drawn to buying one to live in. The large table in the center required togetherness for either a family or guests. The table in the kitchen itself was the hub where Jo gathered with her family and friends and black velvet stanchions had been purchased to keep guests out of that area, reserved for Ginni and family only. Guests were welcome to look but not cross the threshold. Except for Grimm Night Detective who had full access.

281

"Well, it's time. Ready?"

"Let's do this," Maitland said, and Weathers, who sat in the chair on the big table in the dining room in front of the screens with Maitland standing behind him with her hands on his shoulders, hit record. The cameras were now recording ever room and from this point on they could just explore, and the cameras would pick everything up.

They had to begin with a baseline sweep with the K2 meter and get a reading in each room. They started downstairs and as Weathers made a reading in each room, he called out its K2 level and Maitland wrote it down. They did this in every nook and cranny of the livable space, including the rooms upstairs. Although certain areas had elevated readings, normal for electrical in old houses, nothing was out of the ordinary. Again, the Cold Room was scary simply for knowing what it was, and they found themselves moving faster in and out to get the readings in the Cold Room suite, the hallway and the Cold Room itself, and although they felt on edge, nothing happened. The upstairs sweep was also finished.

They closed the Cold Room door and stepped into the Safe Room where they had placed all their stuff. Weathers turned off the K2 for now and threw it on the bed. He then threw his hat and then himself on the bed on his back and laid down for a moment.

Maitland closed the door. She needed to feel she had some privacy and, even, safety, which was odd, being that they were entirely alone in the house. She joined Weathers, placing her hat neatly on the side table and then laid back on the bed staring up at the ceiling and taking a deep breath. It was the first time in hours that they had stopped and taken a break.

"Ah, this feels good on my back," she said.

"Oh, yah," he responded to her and looked at her and smiled.

"Now what should we do?"

He rolled to his side facing her. Both still had their feet off the bed. With their boots on still, they were not rude people and had manners no matter who was looking.

"Well, I know I'm hungry. Let's order some dinner and then explore downstairs a little more," Weathers said.

"Ooh, yah. I'm hungry too." She rolled to her side facing him, pulling one leg up in a modified fetal position, making sure not to put her boots on the bed resting one leg on the other, as they chatted. "I am really curious actually to see downstairs in the basement. We didn't do a K2 reading down there, but I am curious to just take a peek at what Jo was saying about how the light is gobbled up down there in the vastness of the basement. I want to see the laundry chute too. Aren't they so spooky?" and she

283

smiled a childlike smile at Weathers, and he smiled back reaching for her face gently with his huge hand.

"You're so cute," he said lovingly to her. "Ok, before anything we need to eat and I saw Jo had placed different menus in the dining room area. Let's go down and choose something and order delivery. Then we can look around downstairs while we wait, eat, and then let's go into the Cold Room and do a closer look, sit in the suite, use the Frank's Box and see what we get."

They both sat up and Maitland adjusted her bat jacket. "It's kind of cold in here. I guess that's why there are fireplaces, huh?" she asked rhetorically with a smile. They both kept their clothes ready for action, as was their habit, boots and clothing remained on util their work was done because they never knew what was going to happen.

Maitland opened the door and the first thing she saw was the menacing door of the Cold Room. It wasn't that the door was unlike any of the other doors in style, that gave off a feeling of warmth and invitation, it was that the Cold Room door was like a personality, unfriendly, that drove you out, not toward.

"That door gives me the creeps," she said, staring at it. Weathers behind her agreed and they noticed a flickering of candlelight in the hallway. It was now dark

284

outside; sundown had reached them some time ago and made the flickering in the hallways all the more noticeable.

"The gas candle lights are on in the hallway," Maitland said. They both looked at each other stunned and then smiled.

"Cameras," they both said at the same time, beginning to run to the back stairs.

They ran down the stairs and into the dining area and Weathers sat at the control table and rewound the footage to them walking into the room and closing the door. Then fast forwarded it. They both knew Jo could have come in and lit them, but they also knew she would have mentioned it, and they did ask for the whole house to themselves for this reason. Still, owners could do as they pleased and thus the cameras were so important. They ran the footage of their chat on the bed at regular speed, while watching the camera also in the hallway. And just like that every single candle lit simultaneously with a gentle light flickering. A real flame. Jo did not light those gas candles. They were just off one moment, and on the other. That feeling that Maitland had looking at the door was for a reason. Something was just out in the hall and went back into that room. There was something unfriendly behind that door and she felt it. Her body got goose bumps.

"So freaky," she whispered and rubbed her arms, feeling chilled. "We're not sleeping in there, you know." They had talked about doing that but talking about it and being in the house and experiencing it made an impact.

"Oh, fuck no, that would be insanity. I like a good scare, but that's ridiculous."

"Oh, thank God," Maitland said. "I'm down for exploration, but there's no way I'm sleeping in there. Let a true-blue skeptic do that. We believe."

"For sure," Weathers said. He had picked up the menus and began going through them. What do you feel like eating? They looked at the menus and selected. "Ooh, teriyaki?"

"Ooh, yah, vegetable tempura," she said in agreement. They ordered online and could explore downstairs while they waited thirty minutes.

They moved from the table in the dining room to looking in the living room.

"Isn't it amazing how opulently people just lived. It feels like everyone had wallpaper on their walls and libraries in their houses," Maitland said looking around and admiring the drapes, woodwork, furniture, ceiling medallions, and then stopped and turned to him. He had taken a seat on the couch.

"Let's go check out the basement."

286

"Ok," he said, and got up. They both walked through the hallway toward the back of the house. "It is kind of spooky to think that there's a whole dark underworld underneath this house."

"Yah, agreed. I want to see some of it to understand what Jo was saying," Maitland said. They both walked with measured steps with both excitement and trepidation.

When they reached the door to the basement that was right next to the door of the bathroom, Weathers turned the knob and the door creaked open.

"Oh, hell, no!" Weathers said looking down into its dark hungry mouth.

Maitland jumped up and down in excitement.

287

Chapter Forty-Two
To Eat Mortals Souls

"Mait, are you freaking serious? You want to go in there?"

She excitedly continued to jump about and silently raised her eyebrows up and down without saying a word.

"Really?" he sighed and looked at her. He was gonna have to do it for her. " I actually didn't think we'd have time to look at the basement with everything else." He looked back down at the gaping darkness in front of him. "This looks like a place that eats mortal souls."

Maitland giggled and had settled from jumping up and down and they both stood looking down the stairs that disappeared into darkness. It looked terrifying and completely dark beyond the expanse of light shining from the hallway. As Jo said, *it gobbled up light.* Roger that!

Weathers took a deep breath, "Is there a light?" he put his hand beyond the realm of the door and didn't get sucked in, so that was a good start. He felt on the side of the wall on the right for a light switch and then the left, finding none.

"Try up," Maitland said. "Maybe there's a light switch rope like in the closets.

He looked at her and stuck his hand up and fumbled in the air swiping to find something. It was completely dark, and he half expected to get pulled in by some monster, but instead, he found a swaying string and pulled on it. A light turned on.

The light did little to lessen the darkness that lay ahead of them and made it only to what seemed close to the bottom of the stairs but revealing nothing of what lay beyond. There must be another light switch below. *There better be*, Weathers thought to himself. He felt a small comfort in knowing that there had been others down there because they had to do their laundry there, so he shook off his fear of entering the abyss below. Normally he had met these sorts of situations with curiosity, but he had a 'feeling' he didn't like but he was going down there anyway. Maitland wanted to go and that was enough for him. He loved her and if she wanted to do this, they would do it.

"We have to use the handheld; we didn't put cameras down here," he told her.

She already had the camera in the gimbal. She was prepared.

"We need a flashlight. "

She walked through the kitchen and into the dining room where their equipment bags were and grabbed two, one for each of them. They always carried a backup light. Everyone has seen the scary movies where one goes out.

Sufani Weisman-Garza

You gotta have the back up. She walked back to him, placed one in his hand, one in her bat pocket and they both looked down the stairs into the darkness.

RECORD

"Ok, you seriously want to do this? *You* want to go *there*?" and he pointed to the underworld below while looking at the camera and then her.

"Oh, yah," she said again with excitement behind the camera.

"Of course," he said looking at the camera, "she makes me go first," and he laughed. "Mait, please pull a chair over here to this door and block it from shutting. I don't want any funny business." He was truly a little scared. He was, after all, the one who the spirit seemed to mess with, he already knew that, and he just wanted to cover his bases with the door. Jo had also said the spirit liked to slam doors and lock them in closets, so he was thinking ahead.

They entered step by step, lowering themselves to the bottom of the stairs, leaving the door at the top securely open. The light from above shone only on fifteen stairs that they counted, hopefully near the bottom of the stairs. To clear the stairs they continued on below the fifteen. There were at least ten more stairs that had no light. The staircase felt wrong, and abnormally long. That would make twenty-five steps to the bottom.

"This feels really deep," Maitland said, filming. "It's really creepy how it sucks up light and even sound, it feels like. I mean, no one is upstairs, but still, it has a deprivation feeling. Do you feel it?"

"Yah," Weathers said as he focused his steps and held on to the railing, instructing her to do the same. "Be careful here," as they entered the dark area of the basement.

They reached the bottom floor with Weathers' flashlight only, keeping hers as a backup.

"I'm gonna turn my flashlight off and I want you to film how dark it is down here without it."

He turned it off and it was blacker than black as the camera looked into the dark and then panned up the crazy long staircase that made the house opening look way too far away, like the infamous light at the end of the tunnel in near-death experiences. Too far, dangerously so. Weathers pulled his phone out of his pocket and checked for bars.

"Interestingly, there is service so far from this point. We probably should have told Jo we were down here but..." his words fell off. There was no need to be dramatic. Flipping the flashlight back on, he said, "Now, to

291

find a light switch". The flashlights found the washer and dryer and certainly the light would need to be close to the bottom of the stairs as well as the washer and dryer. As Maitland panned around that area, she recorded old furniture and décor, creepy mirrors covered as to not get broken, and lots of cobwebs hanging from above, beyond the little circle the washer, dryer and stored items seemed to make a barrier it seemed, to not cross. It was strange. A string hung in between the washer and dryer and he pulled it.

"Nice," he said happy it turned on without a hitch. He looked back up the stairs toward the house seeing how the light only came so far from the top and said, "Jo definitely must add another light in the middle to light up that dark area." Now that the other light was on it was lit, still feeling like basement lighting, and all the dark cast a strange gold to the lights that were not all that penetrating. Still, there was the feeling of deprivation and lifelessness. It was a cold and damp feeling that added to the misery, but it was to be expected. It was, after all, a basement. He would make a note to tell Jo to put flood lighting down here versus the soft lighting bulbs that didn't do much. He didn't understand how anyone could come down there even to do laundry. He looked up and saw the chute on the left side of the stairs that emptied into a large roller

292

bin. Bin to the left, washer and dryer to the right. Interesting that they weren't together.

Maitland handed him the gimbal holding the camera and he filmed, as she began to inspect the furniture, "Ooh, a gramophone." She was intrigued and looked closely at it. Deep rich mahogany with a copper horn, it had a drawer below it and she pulled to see what was inside. "There's a record in here." She blew away the dust from the turntable and read the album cover, "Van Phillips and His All-Star Orchestra. *It's All Forgotten Now*, 1934." She cranked it up with the handle on the right side and turned the switch. It creaked and groaned, but the top began to move. She took the record out of its sleeve and put it on the turntable and lowered the needle that was still intact, although who knew what condition it was in, or if it would even play. The needle touched the record. The old orchestra music began to play in the dark dampness of the basement with the sounds of vintage crackling that nowadays people put into their soundscapes to mimic the days of old. This was real, not a programmed soundscape and she underestimated how hair-raising it would be while down in the basement with very little light. The hair on the back of her neck rose and she could see that Weathers felt the same air of eeriness.

Sufani Weisman-Garza

"That's pretty ... and fricking harrowing too," Weathers said, and they both laughed. As the music played, Weathers activated the tripod and put it on the washer so he could look around too. The camera could catch them both investigating.

They hovered over the gramophone for a bit and Weathers took her hand to dance like olden times having no idea how to do it, but they tried anyway and she obliged. They kissed and then continued to look around never losing sight that they were in a creepy ol' basement.

"So, what's beyond this little barrier," Weathers asked rhetorically. It literally formed a circle from the wall where the machinery was, outward into a rather small circle keeping anyone from moving deeper in.

"I wonder if Jo did that on purpose to feel safe. You know, not so much keeping herself in, but keeping what's back there out?"

"Interesting observation," Weathers said. "What is back there, though?" He took out his flashlight and all he saw was what looked like cavernous nothingness, the light didn't penetrate much, and he felt he needed to break the circle barrier to be able to see anything more than cobwebs hanging from above over the circle. He understood the layout of the house and knew the basic

294

directions the basement would allow them to travel and so he was curious, although nervous.

"Here, let's move some of this furniture to the left to create a space for us to pass through right here. Just enough. I don't want to do a lot of work to put it back how Jo had it. Just enough to get through," he instructed, and they worked together to create just enough space. Maitland went back to get the tripod, closed it and used the handheld for filming.

They walked straight with Weathers in front filming, as Maitland clutched his jacket to not get separated. The more they walked forward, which should be towards the front of the house, the more there was nothing, not even cobwebs, no furniture, no walls or foundation they could see just deep, penetrating darkness, the floors became dirt, and they heard a sound of dripping water that echoed in a cavernous space, a cave, not a house. This didn't feel right and both were scared into silence but kept moving forward against their instincts.

Maitland kept looking back at the faraway light leading back into the house that was getting fainter the more they moved ahead. They could go back, go back into the house, they *should* go back, but instead, they kept going. "No wonder no one wants to come down here. It feels weird," Maitland said, breaking the silence. Weathers did not reply but stayed focused.

Weathers stopped and Maitland watched him. "This is incredible. I feel like we have been walking for, what? a minute, and I see nothing resembling anything attached to the house. Look how far back the stairs are to the house, surely, we would have hit the front of the house by now," Just then, his flashlight caught a deeper shadow off to the right and when he focused his eyes, it looked like an entrance to something, but what he didn't know? They both focused their stare. It was an entrance like one carved into the ground. Not a doorway or something normal, like one would assume would be there in a basement. They both looked at each other.

"You wanted to come down here," Weathers said to her. She was having serious second thoughts, but it was too late now. He was committed to seeing what was down there. Weathers always saw things through. The deeper in they went, the colder it got and their jackets hardly kept the cold out. She could begin to see Weathers' breath in the flashlight.

Maitland continued to follow closely behind him, more because she was scared to be too far from him in such darkness. If something pulled her away, he could not see her once she was out of the light of his flashlight. She

296

was scared but carried on. Her heart was beating fast and everything in her told her to go back into the house, but it was too late. They had to do this. If someone had been living down here, Jo would never know it. It was so vast and too easy to hide in. But who would have the nerve to live down here? Only a monster could live in such a place. Oh, God, she thought.

"Talk about your unfinished basement," she said, laughing nervously.

They got closer to the cavernous opening and crouched down to go inside it. They walked five steps or so and as soon as they turned the corner of the hollowed-out earth there was a golden light like the one at the stairs and the washer and dryer. It gave off only a small amount of light at first and then as they went deeper and deeper, with each twist and turn the light began to get slightly brighter. They followed the light until they came to a door.

The door was one just like the ones in the house above, nice and fitting, Victorian. His brow furrowed; it was out of place and strange. They no longer had any sense of where they were in the house because it seemed an optical illusion of how far they were. Were they outside the realm of the house in some burrowed underground fortress that was well beneath the grounds, or still under the house? With each twist and turn they made they lost their

297

Sufani Weisman-Garza

bearings of where they were. The same feeling of sound deprivation came back. They heard nothing and felt as though they had become deaf. To lose a sense was frightening. Don't react, don't react, don't react.

Weathers didn't worry about getting back to the house, but more about what was behind this door. Something odd was happening and he didn't like it at all. He was scared and being scared made him angry. He knew he could back track the hollow, and that once out of the hollow trail that led them to this door, they would see the very dim light back towards the stairs. But this door; what the hell was this door? They stood looking at it. Then suddenly, the sound of orchestra music came, and the soundlessness spell was broken. It was the same music that was playing on the gramophone in the laundry room, only, coming from this room.

"Here, let me," Maitland took over, handing him the camera. Whenever one of them would get too stressed, the other took over to give them a break. This job was particularly mind boggling and stressful and because of that Weathers needed a break. She stepped in to go first. They made the exchange and took deep breaths to settle their nerves.

She creaked open the door. It opened to a room, a nice room, and they first came upon a velvet drapery in

298

the doorway creating an entrance, with ambient lighting. It was a study; hardwood floors reflected soft lightning, rich with natural oils beneath their out of place gothic boots. They quietly moved in and looked around having no idea what to expect beyond the drape. There was a man sitting at his desk, writing with his quill pen and ink, soft orchestra music played on the very same gramophone, *It's All Forgotten Now*. A different pocket door leading to the entryway of the house to his study was closed, and they heard the sounds of clattering and voices beyond the door. It sounded like a party. He was fashionably dressed in suit and tie fitting the era of the 1890s and beyond his desk across the room from them, and behind a curtain stood a little girl in hiding, watching him. She tucked in between the window, the long velvet curtain and the bulk of the grandfather clock that stood seven feet tall. The music got louder and unbearably so, but the man showed no response, but kept writing. The girl kept watch on him, like a psychopath watches before they kill. It all felt wrong. They were in the study, but deep under the house, in another time.

They were as silent as mice and across the room as they watched the girl, she saw them, slightly turning her attention from her father to them. She put her finger to her lips as if to say, "Shhh," with no sound, and her grin

299

Sufani Weisman-Garza

became that of an unnatural smile that seemed to continuously be pulling up the sides of her face by some invisible string attached to her mouth, almost touching the corners of her eyes. As they watched in horror they knew where they were, who they were watching and they began to stumble backward, all the while the father remained oblivious to them as the girl moved forward toward them, coming out of her hiding space. Her father was locked in time, but the girl, the girl was not. As she walked toward them, her white dress faded with each step. She became more and more decrepit. Her face became angrier, and they felt like they had walked right into her mouse trap. Her slow steps became a hunt.

Maitland began to run back out of the door, initially knocking into Weathers who almost lost hold of the camera but gathered himself in time to get it and get out. They both crouched, and ran out of the door, *It's All Forgotten Now* blared in their ears, and through the twists and turns of the hollowed tunnel that seemed even longer than when they had entered, they ran like bats out of hell, and almost as blind save for their one flashlight. Eventually they were back out into the cavernous space of the basement, still music blaring, and turned left to run toward the light that thank God, was still there, faintly in the distance; washer, dryer, furniture, fucking gramophone

300

Sufani Weisman-Garza

playing that horrible song that they were now terrified of, and the entrance back into the lesser of evils, the Purdy House. They ran and ran and ran until they heard the song in the distance still playing, *It's all Forgotten Now*, in this chamber that echoed, this house that did not forget a damn thing.

Neither of them once looked back for fear of what they would see, and they ran in step with one another as if tethered together. The flashlight bounced the light as they ran and finally came to the circle boundary and slid through the break they had created. Maitland first and she was in, Weathers was through and turned to push back what they had moved as if that would keep the girl out. No matter how irrational, he did it anyway. He yelled to Maitland to run up the stairs and she darted up the twenty-five stairs and he was shortly behind her. The turntable still spun. When they reached the top, Weathers kicked the chair aside and caught their breath and looked down. Beads of sweat, cold sweat, on their brows. They had just run for their lives.

Their breath became calmer, and they stared below, frozen. As they looked into the mouth of darkness, the abyss that ate souls.

"We left the light on down there, Weathers said.

"And the gramophone," Maitland said.

301

They heard footsteps on the cement below over the faint music and a small figure in a white dress broke the barrier of shadow to come into the dim and now flickering light. No longer looking the part of the monster that chased them out, but still, the monster. She waved her finger as though scolding them, "Tsk, tsk, tsk," for forgetting the light, the gramophone, or was it for being so stupid to walk down there in her darkness? They stood frozen watching. They were paralyzed with fear and couldn't move.

She walked with ease out of the light and back into the shadows. The light flickered and went out. The music fell silent.

They stood and slowly backed away from the basement door and with a tremendous force that whipped their hair, the door slammed in their faces.

They were both trembling and touched each other staring at the basement door, ignited with adrenaline, visibly trembling.

Knock, Knock, Knock. The front door erupted. Door Dash. Their food had arrived.

Teriyaki anyone?

* RECORDING STOPPED*

Sufani Weisman-Garza

Chapter Forty-Three
Yippy Ki Yay

Jo entered the back door at seven the next morning, Ginni would be meeting her there any moment to get food out for their guests' breakfast by eight, and things ready for opening day. Jo would refresh the room that GND stayed in. As she opened the back door, she saw bags piled up in the back entryway. They clearly were ready to get out. Checkout wasn't until eleven. She heard Maitland talking excitedly on her cell phone in the dining room as Weathers came out of the restroom.

"Jo," he said in a friendly, but tired tone.

There was a look on his face she couldn't read. Maitland came around the corner excitedly, clearly having ended her call abruptly.

"Fucking incredible," she said to Jo and hugged her. "You don't even know."

"Are you okay?" Jo took her arms, and they held forearms looking at each other.

"Oh, we're okay, OMG, there is so much … It will *all* be in the video. *Wowah!*"

Weathers seemed shaken still from whatever happened, being quieter than Maitland, pondering something that she didn't yet know.

"Want to tell me anything?" she said turning and breaking away to Weathers.

"No," he said laughing. "I need more time to take all this in. I'm not ready. But I need to get out of this house," he said politely.

"No breakfast?"

"No, I think we'll get some coffee on the way out, and I need to still make a call to Donovan, but I can do that from the car."

She could tell by the look in Maitland's eyes that her man was shaken up and Jo could only imagine what it would take to make him react this way. She almost didn't want to know but knew that eventually she would, when the video came out. She didn't push.

"Let me help you at least with all your things to help you on your way," Jo said politely and where Weather perhaps would not allow her to in some other situation, his desire to get far away from the Purdy House allowed it. Soon they were packed up and in their vehicle and she watched them drive away, hearing their tires crunching gravel and leaves as they drove out into the sunshine that was gracing them on opening day. The sky was blue and the clouds were few.

Sufani Weisman-Garza

"There they go." She couldn't help but feel, as irrational as it was, that the sun was a blessing from having been fed.

As they drove out, Ginni pulled in.

"Seven twenty-nine," Jo said looking at her watch. This girl was excited and punctual, and she smiled. Today was an exciting day. Opening Day!

Just then Layce came out of the cottage, and they all walked together towards the house, up the stairs to the big house, entered the back door and closed the door.

Another day began at the Purdy House.

Jo went to the front door and opened it to let in some fresh air and to check that the front porch looked nice for guests' arrival. She saw a white bag on the porch by the last stair leading to the porch that read Door Dash. She was confused. But she gathered it, to take in and toss out.

Chapter Forty-Four
A Thought to Live By

The day was sunny, although she was getting advice and getting used to Pacific Northwest weather. Better enjoy the sun beams when they come and get used to knowing they don't last or stay away too long. Even in the spring, it could rain like the dickens and then out of nowhere, sun for hours. It also was quite reversed and so far, and from what she had heard, almost felt like her days in Costa Rica with the tropical weather, although perhaps not as exciting or exotic, she viewed Washington State weather the same as she did on that fine vacation; tropical. When she looked at it that way, she could prepare without complaint for any weather ahead. She quite liked it and loved the darker grey days even more. She had had enough bright sun to last her a lifetime and loved the soft ambient glow within the house that made her feel warm and cozy inside while watching and hearing the pelting on the roof and seeing nature water itself in their symbiotic relationship of sun and rain. *All get what they need.* A thought to live by.

A week had passed since Grimm Night Detective had visited, and she hadn't heard a peep from them or seen any upload. They all were impatiently waiting, and it was unusual as they posted nothing since their visit, and

306

she secretly hoped that she had not damaged them in some way by inviting them to her house. She had no idea what happened, since they didn't want to spill the beans that morning while they were there. But that look on Weathers' face, she couldn't read it but knew it wasn't good. It was him she worried about. She hoped he was okay. Although Maitland was invigorated by the experience, Weathers had taken it in a completely different way, and she wasn't yet sure he would be okay after the experience. The last thing she wanted to do was ruin what he had going or somehow lower his self-confidence to go into other places such as hers, if indeed there was one quite like hers.

The week of being open for tours and stays went smoothly. Layce had settled on two tours a night that felt comfortable and being that most of it was in the Cold Room itself it didn't bother the guests, who often were on these tours anyway. Two a day gave them enough time to really answer questions and not feel rushed. She toured for five days having weekends off and loved the theater of it, and taught Hank how to do them so on the two days she took off, Hank could do them and then follow the group out to the shop since she already ran it and knew how to do everything. Since Hank and Layce both knew how to run the shop, the schedule could be as flexible for

307

Hank as she needed, so it all worked out perfectly and everyone was happy.

Lacye was in charge of the spa and tours and worked everything out as things would arise, so Jo didn't have a care in the world. Layce had turned out to be quite the leader, given half the chance to show what she could do, and she did it fabulously. She decided she would do less massage work and gave more to their independent contractor, the massage therapist, who loved it. Jo didn't really know the MT well and only had seen her minimally. She would get to know her more as time went on perhaps. The guests and townspeople were taking advantage of the services, and the schedule was full daily. Lacye seamlessly ran the spa and tours, Ginni ran the catering; every morning she came in and made sure the continental plus was provided, dishware looked elegant and food was quality, while also setting out the daily scones and nibbles she put out in the glass antique cake holders, for guests to come at any hour to self-serve tea, coffee, cookies or scones.

Ginni was beginning to stay more and more in the cottage with Layce and Jo figured it was only a matter of time before she moved in. When Ginni stayed she would go into the big house at night just to check there were still morsels of goodies in the glass containers for guests, still learning the supply and demand that worked best. Ginni cared, she was a real champ. She was the same dedicated gal here that she was at Mamma's. She loved what she did, and it showed.

Even the locals were taking part in the stays and were excited to get an inside look at the house they only ever heard rumors about. For the time being, there were no debacles, no blood, fire or flood. The house was abnormally quiet, suspiciously so. The spa annunciator was on like clockwork and Layce monitored it, but as of yet, there was never a need.

Jo continued to do turn down service and found it therapeutic, except doing the laundry, and reminded herself that she would make the call today to have a service get it every few days. She hated the basement. It was too dark. She kept up on supplies needed, shopping and looked over the overall grounds, upkeep, parking, the neighborhood, the schedule, and was the gracious host and caretaker to all who came in, and for those calling from their rooms to the cottage with questions. Everyone fell into their perfect positions, and she was seeing that her ill fate with the home, and, her life tragedy, well, she had turned the lemons into fine lemonade once more. No one, nothing, would get the better of her or break her spirit.

Sufani Weisman-Garza

She was determined to be happy. She knew she deserved that.

Suddenly Lacye barged in the back door with her laptop open and in hand. "The video is up," she said excitedly, her eyes bulging.

Jo's heart stopped for a moment. She didn't know whether to be excited or scared for what she would see and hear. Weathers hadn't left her mind since she saw his face last. *Why was his face like that? What had he seen?* That was what she was afraid of.

They both met at the private kitchen table and Layce put the computer down and spun it towards her. She took a seat at the table and read the description on their YouTube Video: Channel: Grimm Night Detective

Title: Purdy House| The Cold Room| The Most Terrifying Night of Our Lives. I Will Never Be The Same!

Released four minutes ago, twenty-seven thousand views… and growing with each second.

Jo looked down, finger hovering over the play button, nervous. Layce sat next to her side at the table, having not seen it yet either. Jo clicked it and their faces appeared on the camera. Close up. They were sitting in their own kitchen at the table. This was not what they usually did. Jo's fingers trembled. This was their experience, but her life.

Weathers spoke, his face serious, as it was then. "This video requires some explanation first…"

Sufani Weisman-Garza

Chapter Forty-Five
Purdy House| The Cold Room| The Most Terrifying Night of Our Lives!

"This video requires some explanation first..." his head lowered, and he took his time. He was not smiling or jutting out his knifelike fingers like he normally did when he talked to his viewers. Something in Jo sank. Maitland was holding his arm. Subtle cues that she was comforting him, or rather, he needed comforting. Jo and Layce were glued to the video. Over forty thousand views now. They were watching this, everyone, right now, all seeing it at the same time, together. Jo could do nothing more than watch, listen with her hands in prayer over her mouth. Not worried about the repercussions to the house or business, but with what he would say, rather, what he went through. She had been worried about him since the day he left and now she was about to know why. They both listened and sat still.

"We rolled up to this house like we do any other place we visit," they cut to video coming into the driveway and stopping, as she had seen them do in their SUV, while filming the front side of the house. They showed the footage, then back to them at the table. "We met with the owner, her family and employees who are really also friends," and they smiled at each other for approval. "Really

312

nice people. The owner is a really wonderful woman. Yet it was her own tragedy that brought her to this house, and we have to wonder if it wasn't the house that drew her in to fester in her tragedy, to feed it." He took a deep breath and explained her tragedy. Layce looked at Jo, everyone would now know her experience. She looked down for a moment blank faced, considering that. But it was no secret. She was hiding nothing. Weathers continued and she heard words, "hanging from the closet" ..."sold her home" ... "moved to Gig Harbor" ... "moved in to a home both beautiful and absolutely terrifying".

Layce looked at her sister, checking her face. Jo did not stop watching, her face showed no expression. They would talk after.

He talked about the house through voice over while soft orchestra music played ever so faintly in the background, they continued to flash video they took of the property, beautifully putting together the pieces of the puzzle of time; the walk they did outside, the lush landscaping, the cottage house, recounting the story of the history of the house as they walked through the garden, to the yurt porch, the swing in the garden, the bench, the fountain, them looking up to a room no one knew was there, staring at the tall trees, the sky getting a darker shade of grey the closer they got to entering the house, walking,

313

the camera following Weathers inside the house and then to setting up cameras, doing a baseline reading, all while he talked through voice over about the family, the history, weaving Jo's story into the darkness of the house and how it somehow wanted her there. How she was the one person allowed to discover the truth when it had lain silent and slept for all the others who had owned it. It waited for her. His story telling wove through the horror of discovery and absolute unbelievable paranormal activity, horror of bodies, brutality, to finally, teeth that rained down in the living room. The video panned the incredibly beautiful room and to the ceiling where it occurred. He explained, "beams of light shot down from the ceiling like electricity and anger mixed in a fury, raining teeth, horrible teeth, in numbers impossible, cascading and bouncing off furniture with the sound of hard rain, in the living room, while she watched in horror not believing her eyes," just as Jo had recounted the story. He explained the town's reaction to the news of the murders in the home and to her surprise, the supportive nature of all of Gig Harbor residents embracing her, the shock of the tragedy and her plan to open the home as a Tour and Stay.

(Over two-hundred thousand views…)

314

The camera came back to them in the kitchen close up. All dressed in black. Maitland's hair in neon yellow spilling over her shoulders. Weathers in all black, tattooed arms and gothic skull rings on his fingers in front of the camera.

"But we were not prepared for what happened to us. Because, you see, we were ready to capture a ghost. We were locked and loaded to capture the ghost of this manor, the little serial killer. I get goose bumps just saying that," he looked at Maitland and with his forearm exposed already to the camera, you could see it. She reassured him to keep talking.

"We were ready to enter the infamous Cold Room, (they panned to video they took when on their own of every inch of the Cold Room, including close up shots of stained portions of the wall where the children's bodies hung silently for so long), as we had earlier upon our arrival when Jo showed us the room and told us the horrific story of her discovery."

The camera returned to them. He recounted many of her stories of being thrown, slapped, even the first night how things were moved, and she saw her first apparition, and his own run in with weird phenomena with dust being blown violently into his face and the choking he experienced.

Sufani Weisman-Garza

"We wanted to see if we could coax her out, perhaps use the Frank's box to see if we could get some intelligent conversation with her. But we never got the chance. Not in that room anyway.

(Over six hundred-thousand views…)

Jo was perplexed and hanging on every word he said.

"What happened?" Layce whispered, not taking her eyes off the screen.

(over eight hundred-thousand views…)

"As the cameras will show, we went to the Safe Room," and he explained what that was and why it was called such, "Maitland shut the door and we both took a load off for a minute and decided to eat first, order some food from the menus in the dining room, and then Maitland had the curiosity to go down into the basement." He paused.

"Now, you need to know, we didn't have that on our original plan to explore. There was already way too much house to get to over the span of one night. But curiosity killed the cat. We ordered some teriyaki and found ourselves staring down into the darkness of the

316

basement that was way too dark. Even Jo hates the basement and told us that light gets 'gobbled up' down there and she avoids it. But the laundry chute goes down there so she has to do laundry."

Maitland took over and he took some water. "The first thing we noticed was one, how dark it was, two, how many damn stairs there were. The light didn't shine all the way to the bottom of the stairs but just the first fifteen stairs once we finally got the overhead light on. It was on an overhead pulley."

"What?" Jo said but didn't elaborate, she just continued to clutch her mouth with prayer hands again.

"When we went down the stairs, the bottom half of the stairs were in the dark, we counted an additional ten stairs…"

Jo gasped.

"… that were in the dark and we did have our flashlights. Weathers held his for light as we entered and tried to find the washer and dryer and surely the light would be over them. We had a terrible time finding it. When we did, the chute was on the left and the washer and dryer on the right, but there was a clear barrier in a circle formed in this area, which we both surmised was to help make you feel safe when down there. It's as creepy as

317

hell! I wish I had a stronger way to convey it to you. I can't find the words." She paused.

Weathers took over recounting the bone chilling story of the darkness, the cavernousness, the cold, the confusion and endless walking, the hollow they entered and the terror of what they found, and their panicked sprint out of the hell they were in. The relief of being back in the lesser of evils, the house, and how they got to see the girl both in the room in the hollow, a time warp or recreation of the study in the house they call the library, and that they had been shown a glimmer of her, the girl showing them a moment in time of her watching her father, made more chilling knowing that eventually she killed him. And when they were out and stood at the top of the stairs looking down into the basement once more, she walked into the circle of light from the shadows in the basement, warning them once and for all to not be so stupid as to enter her darkness again, with a smile of a psycho and a "tsk, tsk, tsk" finger gesture, and then back into the shadows, slamming the door in their face; a warning that next time they may not be so lucky. She loved the game, the hunt, the play. She fed off their fear and terror and having fed, she retreated to her darkness.

Jo wondered, *where's the footage?*

"You may be asking," Weather said, "why there is no footage? Well, this may be the most terrifying part of this whole adventure. You see, we placed cameras all over the house to capture everything. So, we will close this video with the footage you won't believe."

Jo's arms both got goose bumps and her breathing was tight. She could only think, *Oh God.*

The screen went to a full bleed, Maitland and Weathers were now only on the black and white screen filmed in landscape view from the control cameras, fast forwarded, as the orchestra music continued to play even louder than before. They took the K2 and did their baseline reading downstairs, something protruded from Weathers' back pocket in the screen but too small to see it. They reached the back stairs and continued upstairs doing the entire baseline reading with Maitland writing in fast motion in and out of every room including the Cold Room. The screen slowed down to regular time as they went into the Safe Room. It recorded their conversation and how they threw themselves on the bed and talked for a few minutes. Then it fast forwarded again.

Weathers pulled out a paper from his back pocket and pressed on his phone and then when done, threw it on the bed. They continued to talk on the bed and then… nothing. Nothing happened. They lay motionless, with their

319

feet off the bed and hovering over the floor facing one another as they had been talking and resting. They lay as the dead on the bed motionless, as thirty minutes later, the camera continued to log time, and the Door Dash driver knocked three times and seemed to be scared of the house when there was no answer and left the bag of food above the last step and ran back to his car and took off. They lay there this way, dead to the world, until sunrise when they stirred, completely disoriented as to how they were both still in their clothes, exactly as they had been before, both scared and discussing something.

A voice over came on explaining what we were seeing, showing them talking and bolting from the bed, confused and then running downstairs to the control center and watching the cameras to see what happened, as they were showing us now, to see their surprise, that they had both not moved all night, but they both had a terrifying experience, both the same exact nightmare? Not likely. The end footage silently filmed them opening the basement door in the daytime, staring down into the abyss and Maitland clutching her mouth. The footage changed to their handheld camera view. The light from the hallways shone down on fifteen steps and the bottom cement floor.

The camera shifted to the black and white control camera showing Weathers reaching up for the light switch string unable to find it, and then looked inside reaching to the right side of the door finding a light switch on the wall that turned the light on. They both looked at each other and then downstairs that lit up all the stairs. They stood there for a minute confused just looking down.

The next footage was in the basement; washer and dryer on the left with the chute all together as it made sense, and various pieces of furniture, and boxes, scattered, cobwebs hanging from the ceiling, furniture, rafters and when flashing the flashlight there was a foundation clearly seen, no more endless, cavernous hollow they had been in, no circular boundary. The camera closed in on a gramophone, with a drawer, with a record inside. Weathers filmed Maitland climbing up the stairs. They stood before the open mouth of the basement, the camera now looking up from the darkness to them inside the house and they closed the door mindfully. The camera returned back to the footage of the real moment of their discovery, as Weathers walked to the control cameras and hit the space bar. The cameras went black.

The video ended with the Orchestral music continuing to play, *It's All Forgotten Now*, low at first and with each gallery image of the opulence of the house, the rich colors, the velvet, the candelabras, the furniture, the gas lights, the drapes, the medallions in the ceiling and

321

chandeliers, the grounds, room by room, the music got louder and louder, until it was unbearable, just as they had experienced. The screen went black and silent, and then slowly faded in with the same soft orchestra music:

Purdy House Stay & Tours

Haunted tours, terrifying stays, in a home of a child serial killer, who may still be in the house!

Grimm Night Detective: "She's definitely still there!"

(Over one- million views…)

"Oh, God, I think I'm gonna throw up," and Jo ran to the bathroom by the stairs, and by the very same basement door.

322

Layce ran after her sister and waited by the door, not resisting the urge to open the basement while she waited for Jo to come out. She counted the steps to the bottom, *fifteen, yes, fifteen to the bottom*, and could only imagine that only ten more steps led them to a hell of a little serial killer's imagination! And not even their unwilling slumber could keep them from it. Not when they were in this house. Perhaps slumber was just another of her means to torture? Not even death had contained her. And oh, how she was about to feed!

Get The First Book In The Series

A Haunting In Gig Harbor

1377 Rikoppe Lane

Book 1

Sufani Weisman-Garza

Acknowledgements

I want to thank the McCall House in Ashland, Oregon, that inspired this entire journey of creating the Purdy House. When my husband and I stayed there several times, we fell in love with the feeling of the living history while being in it, the feeling of being back in time, reading the household ledgers and seeing pictures of the family and even hearing and reading some of their tragic history. We stayed in the room that became Jo's room, that was situated directly across from the 'Cold Room'. The floorplan of the McCall House was the basic foundation of the layout I used in my mind while creating the Purdy House on Rikoppe Lane. The house I chose visually is much larger and foreboding than the McCall house, and of course I embellished and changed many things, while always feeling I truly had been in the house I was writing about, because I had really been in it (minus additional rooms, décor and mysteries I added). I did have breakfast the next morning in the same dining room I recreated with a few guests, one of whom stayed in the room next to ours, and the guest spoke of being kept up by a ghost who was crying all night in her room. In my mind, it became the Crying Room, and this created more inspiration for a thrilling horror story I had just started writing. Although the setting in the book became

325

Gig Harbor, in Washington State, which then borrowed some historical references there, like the name Purdy itself, the inside of the house in my story was all inspired by my stay at the McCall House. Thank you for such an inspiration. I will say that in an interesting way, I was called to the McCall house to write, as I was finishing another book that had been signed by an agent and did some writing there; I have a picture my husband took of me writing there. As I was finishing up the ending of that book. I was called to the McCall house, much in the way Jo was called to the Purdy House; for reasons that unravel over time.

I want to profoundly thank my editor, Carol Trow, for being a warm voice of reason, for fact checking me, for keeping my words meaningful and realistic. I tend to make up words or sometimes have completely different meanings for them until she set me straight. A good editor does more than check grammar, they check that what your characters are doing is what they would do in real life, they check that the facts make sense so it is believable, they question, instruct, are critical as needed and offer support and industry knowledge. I especially appreciate her support while leaving a publisher, re-editing and re-launching the first book. These two books deserved the best edits they

326

could get, and she helped me achieve that. I also want to thank her for being there until we both said we were done. Her support was and is invaluable to me. Thank you so much for all your hours and efforts!

I want to thank my husband for the unending support he gives me and knowing when to carve out undisturbed quiet time for me to write. From one artist to another, he understands me and what being an artist is (because he is one as well, with music) and so he understands the intensity of being in the middle of inspiration and how special that time is. I want to thank him for always understanding and honoring that space. I love him more than words could say!

I want to thank my sister Stacey, for always, and I mean always, being my biggest fan. She has always supported me in all my artistic endeavors and has read pretty much all my writings from the time I began. She has always encouraged me to live my dreams, to go for any inspired idea I've had, and showed up to any and every event I had, to be supportive. She bought my books when I would have given them to her because she wanted to support me. Someone like that is invaluable and I want her to know how much I truly love her (I do tell her all the time of course) and am so appreciative of all her support

327

over the years. I love you, Sissy!

Thank you dear reader for reading this book in any medium, and leaving me a review! I am so grateful for you.

More Books By Sufani

NON-FICTION

TRUE STORIES OF AN URBAN SHAMAN

RENEGADE OF LIGHT

GOOD SHOES IN THE VALLEY

FICTION

PURDY HOUSE| THE COLD ROOM

THE GREAT GATHERING OF GODS

SOUL

THE MANY REALITIES OF LOVE

Sufani Weisman-Garza

About The Author

Sufani is a prolific writer of horror and healing, and usually ties healing into every horror/thriller she writes. Her characters are surprisingly lovable overcoming traumatic experiences and set in terrifying situations. She features strong female characters showcasing humorous sarcasm at times and strong family and community bonds. (Think of her style as Stephen King meets Debbi Macomber)

She lives in Washington State with her husband, fur babies (cat and dog) and amongst the woodland creatures, ducks, birds and squirrels and has been compared to Snow White and Doctor Doolittle. She rescues senior animals.

She runs an online academy in healing, psychology and esoteric practices, with thousands of students worldwide (www.placeofblissacademy.com) and mixes healing with horror, as well as healing non-fiction.

She is a *Star Trek Next Generation* nerd and owns the complete box disc set and watches them over and over again weekly, streams ongoing thrillers, horror and attends horror conventions on a regular basis, oddity shops and weird things to do all around the US.

She's been out of the country one time to Costa Rica and thinks everyone should go out of the country at least once, and she plans to go to more places.

330

She is over fifty, dresses wildly, reads incessantly, mostly indie authors to support them, has grown children and believes the world is just beginning.

331

Sufani Weisman-Garza

Contact & Social Media

Email sufani@placeofblisssanctuary.com

Website: www.placeofblissacademy.com

Facebook: The Imperfect Author| SUFANI WEISMAN-GARZA | Facebook

Instagram: Published Author (@the_imperfect_author_sufaniwg) • Instagram photos and videos

332

333

Sufani Weisman-Garza

Made in the USA
Monee, IL
06 November 2023

45862900R00184